Stilettos In The Sand

Stilettos In The Sand

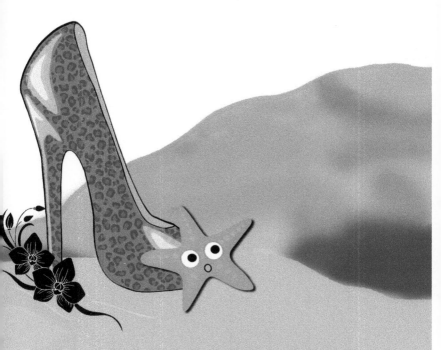

C.L. Bauer

For information contact:

www.clbauer.com

Design: Miller Publishing LLC

ISBN: 978-1-957015-07-1

First Edition: March 2024

10 9 8 7 6 5 4 3 2

The Lily List Mystery Series

The Poppy Drop
The Hibiscus Heist
The Tulip Terror
The Sweet Pea Secret
The Magnolia Dilemma

The Lily List Mystery Exclusives

Stilettos Can Be Murder
Stilettos On The Run
Stilettos In The Sand

Dedication

Never underestimate a good pair of shoes! Our mother loved a beautiful pair of heels. She wasn't flush with money, but she hit every shoe sale with vigor, almost taking on the appearance of a shark during a feeding frenzy.

During World War II, she worked in San Francisco. She walked down Hyde Street to Fisherman's Wharf, and then of course, she walked up the hill back to her small apartment. That workout gave her the best legs!

Here's to Mom, her shoes, and those fantastic legs.

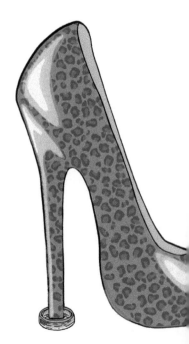

Chapter One

"May I say you know how to treat a lady?" Gretchen Malloy slipped her right foot into one of her high heels. Then she slipped in the left foot and admired the hot pink shoes in the full-length mirror. *My legs are still good. As long as I don't fall and break a hip this old girl has life in her!* Out of the corner of her eye she glanced at Detective Daniel Williams as he covered his bare chest with a starched white custom shirt. *My, my, my!*

Daniel began to finger each button. "You may. I try to treat my woman well."

Gretchen giggled like a schoolgirl. "Trying, dear Daniel is bringing flowers and my favorite wine. Today, we sailed from your private island, checked into this lovely club on Paradise Island, and now we are dressing for a night of elegant feasting and gambling."

Daniel fumbled with his bow tie. "Damn. I never was very good with these things."

Gretchen turned, seeing his frustration. "And that's another reason why you have me! A good event planner knows bow ties, cummerbunds, cufflinks…you name it." She slapped his hand away gently. "Let a professional do this." With her heels on, Gretchen looked directly into his beautiful eyes. "Let me do something for you for once."

As she finished the last touch of the perfect twisting of a necktie, Daniel pulled her body against his. "You've already been doing a lot of somethings for me." He brought his lips closer to hers and gently brushed them before pulling away. "We better go, or we'll lose our reservation."

Gretchen stood motionless. She let out a deep breath and attempted to slow her beating heart. "Daniel, you can't keep teasing me like that," she whispered. "I think you do that on purpose."

"What did you say?" he asked as he pulled his jacket on.

"I said we should go."

Daniel Williams' lips formed a sly smile. "No, you didn't. We can take care of **that** problem of yours later on tonight. I'm starving."

"For food or **that**?" Gretchen arched her left brow. Daniel strode toward her but only grabbed her hand.

"Both, but we have reservations for a lovely meal first. I can tell you what I discovered about our wayward young man over dinner. Then we'll see if we can find him at the hotel."

As he pulled her along, Gretchen didn't mind being led. Daniel's warm hand set her entire body on fire. She hadn't felt this with any man, except for one. In fact, if she told herself the truth, she'd waited for this feeling, perhaps even this one man all her life. *Why couldn't he have met me when I was in my twenties? No. I'm not thinking about that. I have him now. That's enough, actually more than enough for one lifetime.*

After a short ride in the club's chauffeured luxury sedan, they arrived at the resort. Gretchen had visited this place on a business trip a few years back, but that had been business. She'd established strong contacts in several international locations. Even though she planned events in the islands, London, Puerto Rico, Hawaii, and Mexico over the next ten years, she found herself preferring life in Kansas City. Her heart was in the city of fountains, and so she removed all information on her site about international travel to concentrate on her career in the Midwest. Her decision those years ago hadn't failed her. Her business was successful, and she was able to contribute to her community.

Upon arrival at the restaurant and their seating at a table near the water, Gretchen was preoccupied as she searched the space. "I've never eaten here so why does it look so familiar?"

Before Daniel could answer, a very proper waiter stood by their side with a bottle of wine in his hands. "Monsieur Williams, we have your favorite vintner." Another server placed their napkins on their laps and filled their water glasses.

Gretchen reached across the table and touched his hand. "Will I like your favorite wine?"

"I hope so." He looked up at the man and nodded. "Thank you for remembering." A taste was poured for Daniel's approval. "It's as good as ever."

"Wonderful. Will the lady wish for a glass?"

"Yes, of course. Thank you." As soon as their glasses were filled, they toasted each other. "I suppose this is your favorite place?"

Daniel looked over the elegant menu. "I have several, but it always feels very special here."

Gretchen snapped her fingers. "I know! This place was in one of the Queen's special agent movies, just like our hotel."

Daniel smiled. "Give that lady a prize. I thought you'd enjoy coming here for the world class dining and obviously the ambience." He shut his menu softly and placed it on the table.

Gretchen removed her reading glasses from her clutch and was reviewing the elaborate choices. Her eyes caught his. "You can't possibly have read this entire menu, or do you have a favorite you always order?"

"No, I just decide quickly on what I want. Always."

After feeling her heart flutter once more with his obvious intention of dismantling her self-control, Gretchen placed her own menu down. "Really? As I recall when we met you originally thought I murdered one of my clients."

Daniel shook his head. "That was business." He took a quick drink from his glass. "This is pleasure. When I decided I was interested in you, I didn't wait."

"Again, really? You sure drug your heels in the bedroom."

Daniel winked. "But I've been making up for it, haven't I?"

Gretchen Malloy actually blushed. She pretended to look over the menu again. "What should I order?"

"You surely don't want me to order for you."

"You haven't failed me yet. What are we eating?"

Their servers were back, standing as attendants by the table. Daniel looked up and nodded.

"I'll have the Bahamian lobster tail, and the lady will want the pan roasted grouper. Will you choose a shrimp or crab appetizer for us? And we'll both have the French onion soup."

"Very good."

As they walked away, Gretchen turned her attention to the lovely ocean view. "I have a feeling I'll be waddling out of here."

Daniel looked under the table. As he faced her, concern was written on his brow. "Can you walk in those things?"

Gretchen waved her hand in the air. "Please, Daniel. I can run in these things if I have to. Now, what have you discovered about our wayward, supposedly kidnapped young man?"

Daniel relaxed and sat back in the large chair. "Well, you were right, of course. He wasn't kidnapped. He planned the entire thing with a friend of his. Now, all we need to do is find him. He and his friend took a job at the resort, at least that's what I've figured out. I checked in with one of the managers I have known for several years, and the boy was hired two weeks ago, but just started today. I have no idea where he may be living on what little he'll make. He could be sleeping out on King Street."

Gretchen rimmed her wine glass with her finger. "Why would he worry his family like this? Even though they are your caretakers for your home, they seemed more like your friends. Is it just the boy's need for independence?"

"Perhaps. Maybe he's tired of living on a tropical island," Daniel murmured. His thoughts turned to a time when that island was like a prison to him. His parents were arguing day and night about everything including sending their son away to a military prep school. Daniel turned his attention back to his companion. "Living there without friends could become a real problem for a young man. Besides, maybe he has a dream to fulfill."

Gretchen smirked. "You are so nice. Most teenage boys have one dream only and that's to get a girl to go all the way." She raised her glass in the air.

"There is that," Daniel agreed. His glass touched hers in a toast. "I just think his father, Jonah, just never thought his son needed more. I mean, most people would think you were insane if you told them you were tired of living on a Bahamian private island where all you had to do was maintain the property, sail the boat once in a while, fish, and swim."

Gretchen studied his face. Small lines were noticeable around his eyes. His light tan of just a few hours in the sun highlighted them. She hadn't noticed his worry creases before. How could they make him even more handsome, more attractive to her? "Daniel, are we talking about Jonah's son or you?"

Embarrassed at the realization, Daniel's shoulders lifted and fell in a shrug. "Both. I was an ungrateful brat, but that's a story for another time." Thankfully, he was rescued by their appetizer's arrival and saved from a dreary childhood memory shared.

Gretchen's eyes widened as the platter was placed before them. "Oh my. This is lovely."

"Thank you," Daniel said to their server. He looked over the array of jewels from the sea. "What have you brought us?"

"Monsieur Williams, tonight we have fresh oysters with a lemon aioli, prawns with blue crab and gruyere sauce, and fresh calamari and shrimp. There is lemon and garlic for your pleasure. Enjoy."

Before the man departed from the table, Gretchen picked up one of the oysters and slid it down her throat. Her eyes closed as if she was in a trance. "Oh my, my, my. You must have one."

Gretchen didn't see Daniel shake his head. She was such a joy to be around. *Of all the people in the world, Gretchen Malloy is the one I am falling in love with for some reason.* "You know what they say about oysters."

Gretchen's eyes opened quickly, her eyelashes fluttering. "And it's all true, dear Daniel. Maybe you should eat several?"

Her detective laughed as the oyster entered his mouth. "Several? That is good. Later, we'll see if what they say is true, honey."

The French onion soup was divine, and the couple was on their second glasses of wine as they enjoyed their entrees. Gretchen sat back in her chair to gain more air. "That was the most amazing meal I've had in a long time, and on top of it, we have this beautiful view."

"And dessert," Daniel added as a large plate was placed between them. He ordered coffee while Gretchen reviewed the delicacies.

"I'm not sure which one I want." Before her were various samplings including what looked to be a flan and a tart. "What do we have?"

Daniel surveyed the display. He pointed carefully. "This one is a coconut flan, that's a pineapple tart, that's some chocolate thing, and this pink one is guava duff. Why don't we share all of it?"

Gretchen licked her lips. "You know I like sharing!" The dessert eating frenzy began. At the end of the adventure, they drank their coffee quietly.

Daniel paid the charges. Their server left with a large smile on his face. "Now, we should go to the casino, gamble a little, and ask a lot of questions. We may even get lucky and actually spot him."

Gretchen reached for his hand across the table. "Daniel, dear Daniel, I'm not sure why or how you're in my life at this very minute, but I want you to know I'm grateful for you. You know, I've gone for a very long time thinking I was absolutely happy. But now, I realize I wasn't. You make me happy. And for the first time, I'm content and very full."

Daniel winked. "The desserts did you in, didn't they?"

"No, you did me in, very unexpectedly." Gretchen's whisper was barely audible.

"You mean I've vanquished the great Ms. Malloy? I must be amazing."

Gretchen's brow furrowed. "Don't get too full of yourself. Pride makes you ugly, and I should know."

Daniel stood quickly and came around to her. "Let's go." Leaning down, he kissed her cheek sweetly and moved her chair. "I'd like to get back to our suite and see if those oysters work or have really good publicity."

Gretchen stood, brushing her body against him. "I'm sure you don't need the oysters, but verification could be fun. Let's gamble."

I'm not sure who or what we're gambling on. But he followed behind. He noticed the clicking of her heels on the marble floors. The sound gained her attention that was due to her. Men, even if they were with another woman, stopped what they were doing and watched her hips sway through the hall toward the casino. It seemed as though she was oblivious to the attention. *But knowing Gretchen as I do, she knows exactly who is watching. And she loves it.*

"What is your game?" Daniel asked as they entered the gaming hall.

"Blackjack. What's yours?"

"Poker, but tonight I'll just watch you."

Gretchen grabbed onto his arm and began to lead him to the tables. "So you're more of a poker at a dining room table with five or six other cops, beer, and chicken wings player?"

He patted her hand. "You know it. This is too nice and very expensive. I want to move around the room and gain information. You enjoy yourself."

Gretchen continued toward a table with an empty seat. "I can gain intel at a table too, Daniel." The dealer nodded to her. "Do I need a marker, cash, what?"

He patted her shoulder. "I'll take care of it. I have an account. Daniel Williams Esquire. The lady has five hundred to play."

"Dollars?" Gretchen's voice raised in shock. "Dear Daniel, I'll pay you back."

"Sure, I'm just spotting you. He'll tell you when you're close to bust."

Gretchen patted his chest. "Silly, I won't be losing. I'll be fine here. Go do your detective thing."

"And you'll do yours in your own way," Daniel said through clenched teeth. Ironically, he knew that she'd end up knowing more than he did by the end of the night. *Hell, the runaway Isaac will probably be sitting next to her when I return.*

After an hour away, Daniel did have some pieces of information and confirmation that Isaac, Jonah's only son, was working at the resort. His thoughts were of Jonah and Mabel's worries about their boy, missing in the very big, bad world. Daniel owed them. The couple had been a true gift when they came to work for him. Their reliability and passion to maintain his home and the island in excellent condition was unsurpassed. They weren't like family; they were his family. He had to find their son. Daniel heard the commotion as he neared Gretchen. He saw her arms fly up in celebration. Cheers emanated from onlookers.

He shook his head. *What has she done now?* A tray of beers was offered to him, and he grabbed one. He took a large swig. Now, he was ready. He moved his way through the crowd until he stood behind her. Automatically, she looked up at him.

"Daniel, dear. I've been having a glorious time with my new friends." Gretchen began to motion to the three men and two women around the table. "We have Inez and her husband Domingo. They're from the divine city of Seville in Spain. Next to them are Carol and Montgomery Sallers from London. Glorious place. This gentleman next to me is Cyrus. He has a ranch outside of Houston. Have you ever seen a longhorn, Daniel? Cyrus invited us to visit. We could go on a cattle drive. Wouldn't that be fabulous?"

Poor Cyrus lowered his head. "Gretchen, I'm not sure the drive would be a good fit for you," the man commented, his strong Texas accent pouring over his words.

Gretchen placed both hands on her hips. "I'm very good in the saddle."

Daniel had just taken another drink from his beer and heroically managed every muscle to not spit it out onto her hair. Everyone else at the table laughed outrageously. Even the dealer broke a smile.

"You all have very dirty minds," Gretchen said playfully. "I believe I'm finished for the night. Cash me out, Andres." She threw a large denomination chip in his direction.

"Yes, Madame and thank you." Quickly, he gathered her chips and handed her a printed receipt. "You will cash out at the window, Madame Gretchen."

"Thank you so much. It was a delightful evening." Gretchen swung her legs around.

The rancher pointed down at her footwear. "Can you walk in those heels, Gretchen?"

She kissed him on the cheek leaving a bit of hot pink lipstick on his cheek. "I do just about everything in heels." Gretchen added a wink and placed her arm around Daniel's waist. "I have to get this little boy to bed. Tootles."

As she stood, Daniel kissed her soundly on the lips. One of her ankles buckled, but he caught her with one arm while still holding his beer. "And I'll take you to bed too. Good evening, everyone." The cheers and laughter from the crowd could still be heard as they walked away.

Daniel followed his companion quietly to the window. "I'd like five hundred dollars to be placed into Mr. Williams' account, please. I'll take the rest with me."

"You don't have to do that, Gretchen," Daniel said as he leaned against the wall. "You should keep a few dollars. You can't have that much leftover."

"I don't want to be a kept woman. I never have been, and I'm not about to begin now."

"Madame, you want all of the winnings in cash? We could place the money in your account."

Gretchen shook her head. "I don't have an account."

Daniel, suddenly interested, straightened up and leaned in. "How much does Madame have left after you place the five hundred dollars into the account?"

"Five thousand."

"Dollars?" His voice broke as he said the word.

"Yes, American dollars. The cash might be dangerous?"

Daniel held up his finger. "Wait just a second." He dropped his head to Gretchen's. "You won five thousand dollars?"

"And the five hundred dollars you spotted me that you now have returned to your account." Gretchen's smile widened. "I told you I was very good at blackjack. Will the cash be a problem?"

Daniel tried to remember the rules about cash when entering back into the United States. Customs was always suspicious of everything, especially when you were returning from the Bahamas on a private plane. "How about this...let's put it into my account, and I'll write you a check when we get back to the island?

Gretchen thought for a second. "Um, that will work. Yes, please keep it all in Mr. Williams' account. Thank you. I'd like a receipt, please."

"Certainly, Madame."

Gretchen fell into Daniel's body as they waited at the window. "I think the oysters are beginning to do their magic." She nuzzled her nose against his chin.

Daniel's arm draped over her back. "Are they now? Lucky for me, I have a car waiting outside. We can be back in the room in five minutes."

Gretchen smiled. "Lucky for me." She placed her head on his shoulder and spotted the young man holding a tray of Bahama Mamas. "Isaac."

Daniel patted his lady's back. "We will look again tomorrow."

"No, Isaac," Gretchen said as she pulled out of his embrace, grabbed her receipt for the deposit quickly, and began to walk away. She turned back at him. "Keep up, Daniel. We are on the trail."

"What happened to the oyster magic?" Daniel asked as he followed behind her quick steps.

Gretchen patted the air with her hand. "They're highly overrated. He's here. Look." She pointed to the server in the corner.

"I'll be damn. It's Isaac." He began to stalk toward him, but Gretchen stopped his motion.

"I'll go. If you head over there, he'll rabbit."

As his companion sauntered toward the young man, Daniel grabbed his head. "Rabbit? Where does she get this stuff?" *But, she's right. If Isaac sees me, he'll vanish.* Daniel stepped over into a corner of the casino as Gretchen approached the runaway. If things went very wrong, he could possibly catch him as he ran by.

"Excuse me, could I have one of those?" Gretchen asked as she approached the server. She took a drink off of the tray before the boy looked up to see the almost familiar face. She could see the confusion in his eyes. "Now, look, let's keep this calm. What are you doing here? You're worrying your family for no reason."

"You're Mister Daniel's friend."

"I am." Gretchen added a soft smile and nonchalantly took a drink. The cocktail was way too sweet for her taste. *Lily would love something like this. My friend would probably want an umbrella with her pineapple spear and cherry.*

"What are you doing here?"

"Well, I'm enjoying myself, and you're working. Now that we've established our places in this life at this time, let me suggest you stop running, call your parents, and tell them where you are. They are worried and very upset, and that little kidnapping ruse was very minor league. You could've done better than that. Besides, you look like you haven't slept since you left the island."

The young man stared at the woman, blinked several times, and shrugged. "You don't know me."

"I know a coward when I see one. I was you centuries ago. I ran away when I should've stayed and dealt with my problems."

"It worked for you," Isaac interjected quickly.

Gretchen laughed and took another sip of her drink. "Not really. It took me years to correct the situation."

"I don't understand."

Shaking her head, Gretchen placed the drink on a nearby table. "No, you don't, not now. I didn't either. You see, I ran away from a great love. I felt hurt, and instead of staying and talking out our problems, I ran away. It cost me love and so many lost hours of sleep. I looked worse than you. I know it's hard to believe that I could look awful, but I did back then. Obviously, I've overcorrected." *I certainly hope he's listening to me because I really don't want to go into any more detail. It hurts too much.*

"I've made my decision."

"To do what?" Gretchen pointed at the tray. "Do you want to be a server? Is this the life you really want?"

"No. I want to be a marine biologist."

"Well, you're not going to do it in this casino. You need stability. You need more education, and you need dedication. You're not going anywhere here."

"But—"

"But, you don't have a plan. You and your little friend came up with this poorly managed idea. You need to put that tray down and go home."

"But—"

"But nothing. Stop being a coward. Suck it up, buttercup."

Isaac placed the full tray of drinks down on a table and sat down in a nearby chair. Daniel watched suspiciously as the scene played out. *What was the boy going to do now?*

"I have been sleeping on the beach," Isaac muttered. Gretchen sat next to him and grabbed his hand.

"Come back with us, and tomorrow we will take you home. You should speak to Daniel about your dream, your ambitions. Maybe he can help you? And you need to see your parents. They deserve a son who will face them and tell them the truth. You deserve it for yourself. Trust me."

Isaac studied his hand in Mr. Daniel's lady's jeweled fingers. "What did you do after you left?"

"I worked. I loved my family, and I threw myself into my dream. I sacrificed love, but I've been very fortunate. I'm not afraid anymore, Isaac." Gretchen looked over at the detective watching her every move. "I have everything now that I've stopped being afraid." Gretchen withdrew her hand and patted Isaac's. "So what is it going to be the tray or the truth?"

"I want to go home."

Gretchen stood up quickly. "Good. Let's get you out of this job now, and we have a couch you can sleep on if you promise to still be with us in the morning."

"I promise," Isaac answered slowly. "Will Mr. Daniel help me?"

"I'm sure he will, but you'll have to apologize for your absurd ruse."

The boy appeared confused. "I don't understand."

"For your idiot idea, got it?"

"Yes, Madame."

Gretchen motioned for Daniel to come over. "We need to get him out of this job, and we're taking him back to our place for the night."

Daniel Williams agreed. *So much for those mystical, magical oysters.* "Sure. Let's talk to the manager. Let's go, Isaac."

"I'm sorry, Mr. Daniel," the young man murmured as they headed behind the employees' door.

"You only need to apologize to your parents. They've been worried sick about you. I'll call your father when we return to the hotel. Maybe that'll cushion it for you a bit."

Gretchen remained silent as she followed. It was Daniel's turn to take the reins. Obviously, he was known at the casino. He'd have some pull with the management.

Less than an hour later, Isaac was in his own clothes, his job had been terminated, and he had been given the money he was due. In silence, they returned to the resort suite, and Daniel set up the couch with a pillow and blanket.

He pointed at the couch. "You will be in this suite in the morning. If you aren't, I'll track you down and make sure you pay for my inconvenience. Is that understood, Isaac?"

"Yes, Mr. Daniel."

"Good." Daniel clapped his hands. "We'll be in the other room. If you need anything, knock at the door. I'm calling your father in a few minutes. Do you want me to tell him anything?"

"Tell him…tell him I'm sorry." Isaac's head hung down as he stood by the couch. Daniel hung his arm around the young man's shoulders.

"Isaac, you are better than this. I'll help you in any way I can. I understand wanting more, being more. We'll talk in the morning. Goodnight."

Gretchen watched with rapt attention. *How can I possibly love this man even more?* As Daniel walked by her, he grasped her hand and led her away. She waved back at Isaac and blew him a kiss goodnight.

Once behind their closed door, Daniel pulled her into his arms for a long kiss. "Those nice little oysters are going to go to waste tonight."

Gretchen's brow raised quizzically. "And why is that, sir? The bathroom is completely soundproof."

Daniel grinned. "And how do you know that?"

"Because, dear man," Gretchen said as she wrapped her arms tightly around his waist, "you didn't complain about my singing."

"Well about that…I'm deaf in one ear." His laughter was received with a hard shove.

"Come with me, Detective Williams." Gretchen crooked her finger to beckon her man toward the bathroom. "I have plans for you."

Daniel shook his head. "I'm sure you do, but I need to make one call first, and then I'll be in. Warm the water for me."

Gretchen kicked her stilettos in his direction. "Make that call a fast one." She began unzipping her dress as she walked away.

And now he needed to assure a very worried father that his son would be home by tomorrow afternoon. He also needed to make sure a young man was set on the proper course to become a marine biologist. Isaac wanted to study stingrays and their filtration system. Daniel shook his head. It would be simple enough if Isaac applied himself to his studies and went to good schools.

"This is an easy one. All I wanted to do was save the world," Daniel admitted out loud. He could hear Gretchen singing. He needed to make this phone call a very short one. Those pesky oysters' power seemingly was not overrated.

Chapter Two

"Daniel, don't you have to be at work by nine?"

Gretchen attached her second earring as she walked briskly past her bed and the very handsome man who was still laying in it.

"I have plenty of time. Besides, I like to watch you get ready in the morning. Where are you going this early on a Tuesday? We just returned Sunday night from the Bahamas." Daniel stretched slowly. He looked past Gretchen to see the bedroom window of her apartment. Snow was beginning to stick on her balcony.

"Mrs. Notte wants me to drop by. She left a message yesterday, and I promised."

Daniel patted the pillow next to him. "You promised me a morning treat. Come back to bed."

Gretchen shoved on her blazer and fluffed the back of her hair. "The treat I was referring to were your favorite muffins that are waiting for you in the kitchen. She's providing breakfast for me." As she glanced back at the man in her bed, Gretchen smiled. Daniel's bare chest was completely visible. The sheet at his waist revealed his tanned physique. *I'd rather get in that bed, but I have to go. When a woman of Mrs. Notte's stature in the community summoned you, you presented yourself on time.*

Gretchen grabbed her purse and threw her phone inside. She pointed back at her man. "You, go to work. Save our city." She leaned over and quickly gave him a peck on the check. "I will see you tonight. I'm cooking so be here by seven if you know what's good for you, Detective."

Daniel saluted. "Yes, Gretchen. Seven. Be careful out there. We aren't on the island anymore."

"I promise. I'm always careful. I'll visit and return back here to work. You, mister, be safe."

Gretchen's hips swayed as she began to leave the room.

"Gretchen."

Turning back, the elite event planner smiled sweetly. "Now what, Daniel?"

"Gretchen, I love you."

Why did he have to say that? He's said it before; I've said it before, but are we becoming too comfortable? This sounded serious. What about the future? Isn't it time he left me? Gretchen gulped. Taking a deep breath, she threw her head back and laughed. "Of course you do, Daniel. And why wouldn't you?" As she left, she heard his laughter. She dodged a bullet this time. On his private island they had said words of love, but that was there. Anyone can be romantic and say things they don't really mean when they have the sun up above and their feet in the sand.

Gretchen winced in the elevator. "Dang ankle." An old injury always reared its ugly, painful head when she was barefoot too long. Now that she was wearing boots with the most beautiful leopard print heels, she was regretting her lack of footwear on most days of their trip.

"I should have just worn my heels in the sand."

By the time she drove the couple of miles to the stately home off of Ward Parkway, the snow was beginning to add up. The usual five-minute trip tripled in time. She stood at the massive front door and was greeted by Mrs. Notte's trusted butler and assistant, Barrett.

"Ms. Malloy, how nice to see you again."

He took her coat and led her to the grand dame. "It's lovely to see you as well. When the dear lady calls, I come."

"And how is our Lily?"

"Lily is with her husband and two children in Virginia. She's very happy."

"The baby girl is doing well?"

"Yes. How are you?"

"Well, but Mrs. Notte is concerned. I'm worried about her. I hope you can help."

Gretchen nodded as she was led into the beautifully decorated dining room. Mrs. Notte sat at the head of the long table. There was a simple flower arrangement of tulips in front of her plate. The elderly woman waved and pointed at the seat on her right.

"I'm so happy you're here, Ms. Malloy. I hope you love a good breakfast. I was famished this morning."

Gretchen took her seat as Barrett poured her coffee into the exquisite china cup. He vanished quickly. "Breakfast is my favorite meal. How are you?"

Mrs. Notte's smile vanished. "Distracted, yes distracted. I'm worried, dear."

"What is troubling you? And how can I help?"

"I believe someone is trying to kill me."

Gretchen nearly choked on her coffee. "Excuse me?"

"They're trying to do me in. I just know it." Mrs. Notte took a leisurely drink from her cup.

Gretchen said nothing. The Notte family had a sordid past. The woman's own grandson was a drug dealer and murderer, and her very own son Bernard had been involved in art thefts and his own troubles with the drug trade. Money was always at the root of it. It was odd since the Notte family was well off and was a pillar in the Kansas City community.

"Who would want you dead?"

Mrs. Notte scoffed. "There's a list of several suspects. Even though my son and grandson are both in prison, I can imagine them hiring a hitman to do the job. Then there's other members of my family. They all need money. The young people just don't know how to work or handle their dollars. I've lived far beyond my life expectancy as far as they are concerned."

"That's ridiculous. I'm not sure what our world would be without you, Mrs. Notte," Gretchen said with a smile. She patted the woman's hand. "Lily would be absolutely inconsolable. She respects you so much."

"I miss her, don't you?"

Gretchen's smile faded. *I miss her more than I should. She's almost like a sister.* Her thoughts turned to her own sibling, Amy who had died a lifetime ago. "Every day, but a girl has to work, make a living so I keep myself busy."

As Barrett placed breakfast in front of them, Mrs. Notte winked. "And I bet that handsome detective gives you a run for your money."

Gretchen unexpectedly giggled as her thoughts turned to the naked man she'd left in her bed less than thirty minutes ago. "He keeps me busy as well."

"You are very fortunate to have found each other. Now, let's put all depressing thoughts aside and eat." Both women began to enjoy their eggs Benedict and fruit.

At the end of the meal, Gretchen poured coffee into both of their cups. "Now, what can I do for you?"

"I have a list of suspects, and I have a list of what I need to do. If you'd assist me in this endeavor, I will make sure it is worth your while."

Gretchen shook her head. "No, you will not. I'll be happy to do anything for you."

Mrs. Notte clapped loudly. "That's why I called you. There aren't many honest people left. I have you and Barrett." She reached over and landed her hand atop Gretchen's. "And, if I die, just know I've lived a remarkable life. I wouldn't have done anything differently except–"

Gretchen watched as Mrs. Notte's eyes looked away. "I would've locked my son and grandson away in a dungeon…if I had one."

"There's always a bad apple or two in every family."

Mrs. Notte stood up and grasped the cane in her left hand. "I seem to have enough to make pies. Let me show you what's been going on." Gretchen followed behind, enjoying the tour past several pieces of art that would catch a small fortune at auction.

The elderly woman stopped in front of a small window. Her pointed finger directed Gretchen's attention. "Here is a bullet hole. I usually sit in front of this window every day around six and read my newspaper, that's six in the morning just after it has been delivered."

Who still had a newspaper delivered? Gretchen leaned down. It did appear to be a hole that could've been created by a bullet. She quickly removed her phone from her purse and shot a couple of photos. She'd have Daniel take a look tonight. She looked up to see the homeowner continuing down the long hallway.

"Then, there's this." She pointed down at smudged marks on the floor near the double French doors leading out to the patio. "Someone made these, and it wasn't me or Barrett." Mrs. Notte looked out at the winter scene. "Oh my, Ms. Malloy. I didn't realize how snowy it had become. Will you be able to drive home safely?"

Gretchen nodded. "I'm a great snow driver. Don't you worry. Are you sure maybe a delivery man or repair person didn't use this side door recently?"

"Absolutely not!" Mrs. Notte was adamant. "No one comes through this entrance during the winter. Those marks weren't there two days ago."

Instead of furthering any argument to Mrs. Notte's proclamation, Gretchen just nodded. "So, we have a bullet hole and smudge marks on the floor. Anything else?"

"I suppose the note might be helpful, and then there's the prescription mistake two weeks ago, and the car slowly driving past the house for the last month. It's red. You'll have to ask Barrett for the make and model. He's seen it too. He told the police after the alarm system was set off, but they thought it was students out for a joyride…every single night."

"My, there does seem to be something going on."

"I want this to stop, and if it means that we must fake my death to solve this mystery, I'm up for it. You know I assisted in the arrest of a notorious drug facilitator. Devlin, Lily, Carlos and several other good looking men were involved, but I did my part. There's even that handsome priest who could make me convert after all of these years."

Gretchen hid her delight by glancing away to look out at the winter storm. *Yes, Devlin's handsome priest friend Dan could make you change your mind about your own faith. It seemed all the good-looking men were named Daniel!*

"Ms. Malloy, I have everything you need in my office. Come this way."

Seated at a round table in what used to be Mrs. Notte's husband's wood paneled office, the two women aided by Barrett examined all of the written evidence.

"Barrett, have you noticed anything amiss?" Gretchen asked as she looked over the compiled list of suspects.

The faithful employee glanced over at his much-loved employer. She nodded, giving him the permission he needed. "The mistaken prescriptions could've been fatal. I caught the problem. The pharmacist knew nothing about it. Then, the note that you're reviewing right now was rather chilling. At first, I just thought it was an awful prank, but now–"

"Well, after you receive three of them, with the threat that if you don't die soon, they'll kill you, you do take notice." Mrs. Notte sniffed in the air as though the entire idea of her demise was distasteful.

"And, Ms. Malloy, we've had some rather disturbing telephone calls on the landline."

Who still had a landline? "I see. What were they about?"

"Some breathing, some cursing, and definitely threatening. The threats against my lady's life have been consistent for a month now."

Gretchen compiled all of the written information. "May I take these with me?"

Mrs. Notte nodded. "You have the copies. The originals are in my safe here in the office."

"It seems like you're prepared to fight this," Gretchen suggested.

"Of course. I have a great granddaughter and a family to enjoy. I won't give up on them now that I've found them."

Mrs. Notte had been denied even knowing of the existence of a great granddaughter for years. She enjoyed the girl's mother and stepfather Carlos who worked with Devlin Pierce in the DEA. They were the elderly woman's family now.

Gretchen stood to leave. "I'll try in any way I can, Mrs. Notte. I'll keep in touch with you and Barrett. I better go. It looks like the weather is deteriorating." All three took a glance out of the window. Gretchen could barely see her car in the driveway. "Please take care of yourself." When she leaned down to shake Mrs. Notte's hand, the elderly woman pressed her arms around her.

"Thank you so much. I didn't know who else to turn to."

"I'll show you out," Barrett said as he led the visitor to the front door. "Ms. Malloy, I've never seen her this upset. The police won't do a thing, and frankly, I'm not sure they believe us."

"Are you afraid, Barrett?"

The stalwart assistant nodded. "I am, for her."

Understanding, Gretchen nodded. "Is there anyone on these lists that **you** suspect?"

"Actually, there's several including a former employee, Mrs. Notte's own sister-in-law, a niece, a great niece, two boys who used to help with the lawn…"

Gretchen patted his arm in comfort. "So, there's a few from over the years?"

"The lady has lived a long life. I know she has a hard exterior, but she is one of the best people in this world."

Gretchen appreciated his sentiment. Her own Daniel used to think she was a murderer, and then he realized she had so many attributes that were so very complimentary, he couldn't resist her. "I'll be in touch."

The short drive home seemed endless. Gretchen stopped by for a few groceries and hurried–as much as you could as you avoided sliding cars–back to her apartment. She had an afternoon's worth of emails and messages from clients. She stopped working around four and made an overdue phone call.

"Lily? Are you there?" All Gretchen heard was a little boy singing and a crying baby.

"No, yes."

"Drew? Is this my little Drew?" Lily's toddler had answered the cell phone.

"Andrew. Auntie G?"

Gretchen clutched at her heart. *I must send that little angel a gift. I wonder if I can order a pony, and have it delivered?* "It is Auntie G. Is your sister having a bad day?"

"Bad day today."

"Andrew, give mommy the phone. Gretchen? Are you there?"

"Yes, Lily. Your son and I were having a lovely conversation. He is so smart."

Lily Pierce, former Kansas City florist, was dealing with a newborn and a toddler who insisted he knew better when it came to what to wear, eat, and when to take a nap. "He's only around adults. I saw on the weather channel that you have a snowstorm."

Gretchen looked out her balcony and saw nothing. Only days ago, her feet were in warm sand. "It is a big one. I'm calling because I visited Mrs. Notte this morning. She's having problems."

"Dev spoke with Carlos the other day, and he said her heart is causing her some discomfort. They're thinking about a pacemaker?"

"She didn't mention anything about that. She believes someone is trying to kill her."

Lily chuckled. "Gretchen, she may need some attention. She misses Angelica so much. She loves that little girl."

"Mrs. Notte did mention that, but I believe her, Lily. She gave me evidence, and I even saw a bullet hole in one of the windows."

"Andrew, please don't put your finger up your nose," Lily directed her son. "A bullet hole? She should call the police."

"She did." Gretchen pulled out her defrosted chicken and a frozen bag of vegetables. "They did nothing. I have the evidence. I'm going to have Daniel look at it, but I'm going to do a little digging as well."

On the other side of the line, the frazzled and sleep deprived friend in Virginia rolled her eyes. "Gretchen, you know you shouldn't do that."

"And why not? If you were here, we would be doing it together."

Lily shook her head in an exaggerated fashion causing her son to laugh out loud. "Maybe, but I have this feeling Mrs. Notte just needs your company. You used to think she was a stuck-up old fart as I recall."

"That's when I did that one and only event for her over a decade ago. She was a pain and very demanding, but over the years, she has had her share of tragedy. I want to help her, and you know I'm quite good at undercover work."

Lily stuck her tongue out at her toddler. "Your undercover work is a bit different than what most people understand it to be."

"My, my, don't you have a dirty mind. I am speaking about my investigative skills, but I'm very good at the other. You can ask my detective."

Poor Daniel! "Yes, Gretchen, I have no doubt about that. Crud. I have to go. Andrew is pouring the flour out–"

"Well, that's just silly. Lily? Lily?" Gretchen stared at her phone. "She hung up on me. Lily Pierce! Have you lost your mind?" *She probably has because of those two little ones. I need to plan a trip…after the baby is a little older. I'm not sure a baby does well with a day of shopping.*

Gretchen began to prepare dinner, cooking her chicken, making her sauce, and putting it all together to bake in the oven. If she planned it just right, the chicken pot pie would be a lovely flaky golden brown as Daniel walked into the apartment. She added a mixed salad and a side of parmesan-baked green beans.

It's one of his favorite meals. Hopefully, I'll get the answers I need when he has a full stomach and has his feet up while I massage his neck. It usually works–

Chapter Three

Gretchen lifted the pie out of the oven as she heard the door open. "You have perfect timing, darling."

Detective Daniel Williams' long day suddenly became a distant memory. "You usually say that about me." He threw his keys and coat on the hall table and began to struggle with his tie. He threw it onto the stack. "It smells good."

"It's your favorite...chicken pot pie. I even made the crust from scratch."

Daniel stopped. *My favorite? Why? She only does this when–* "How was your day? The roads are dangerous."

"I was in the apartment before lunch. Get comfy on the couch. I'll serve you there. Beer, wine, or something else?"

"Coffee. I'm freezing." Daniel plopped down and kicked off his shoes. *Yes, she needs something. It's always fun to figure it out.* "I can help you."

"No, no, no. I have everything. You've had a long day, darling. Just rest. I have coffee brewing." Gretchen walked over two plates of salad and arranged them on the coffee table. "I'll be back with the entree and green beans."

Daniel reviewed the perfectly plated salad, complete with chopped nuts and Gretchen's homemade pomegranate dressing. His brows furrowed as he observed her in the kitchen. She was wearing a soft fuzzy sweater that accented both of her best features, tightly hanging in all the right places over leggings. Her bare feet slapped on the tile as she slipped over to the living room. She had sliced an enormous serving for him, and he could see the steam releasing from the pot pie.

"What did I do to deserve all of this?"

Gretchen sat across from him in a large lounge chair. "After the lovely trip you gave me, cooking for you is the least I can do."

Now Daniel was definitely suspicious. He cocked his head and decided he would eat first before he'd question her behavior. When Gretchen cooked, she was firmly in her element. Daniel relished each and every bite.

Nearly an hour later, the meal was completed and the chit chat had begun to focus on Mrs. Notte and the breakfast visit.

"So, she's in good health?" Daniel asked as he began to load the dishwasher.

"Yes and no. She's distraught. Yes, that's the word."

Daniel laughed. "Honey, I've never found you to be at a loss for words. Spill."

"Spill what?"

"Gretchen, this meal was lovely, and I do appreciate it especially after the day I've had, but I know you. What do you want?"

Gretchen stepped back, clutching her throat. "How dare you think that I did all of this just to get something from you. I love making that salad dressing and the crust from scratch. I don't mind spending my entire afternoon mixing up one of your favorite meals–"

Daniel stood straight up and turned on the dishwasher. "And what's for dessert?"

"I made your favorite, chocolate cream pie–"

"From scratch?" Daniel crossed his arms across his chest. "I rest my case." As he passed by the woman in his life, he gave her a quick peck on the check. "You are very predictable, and very beautiful."

Gretchen began to complain, but instead smiled sweetly. She loved it when he said she was beautiful. She even loved the predictable adjective. Throwing her hands up, she walked back into the living area. Instead of resting in the chair, she sat next to him on the couch.

"Fine, I need some of your expert assistance."

Daniel motioned for her feet, and she happily splayed them across his lap. Detective Williams had magic fingers. He knew it, and Gretchen definitely knew it. "Tell me. What's going on with Mrs. Notte?"

Gretchen leaned over and unbuttoned his shirt. "That's better. You look more relaxed now."

"Do I get dessert before or after you tell me?"

Gretchen sighed and not in a good way. "Fine. Dessert after I tell you. She thinks someone is trying to kill her. I saw a bullet hole in the window where she usually reads her newspaper. I took photos of the evidence."

Daniel concentrated on Gretchen's left ankle, kneading the tight muscle a little harder. "Who reads a newspaper?"

"Mrs. Notte does at six in the morning. Pay attention. I saw some marks on the floor coming from the patio doors, the private patio doors which access the private garden. I'll have you look at those photos too."

"Obviously, someone forgot that the butler or a maintenance person went out or came in through the doors. It's winter–"

"So, they were checking the central air unit outside? No."

"Fine. Did they have an inspection from the city? From one of the utilities?"

Gretchen slapped playfully at his arm. "Must you be so pragmatic?"

"I must. Wow, your ankles are really tight."

"It was my boots today. They're very expensive and very bad on my feet. But they are so magnificent."

Daniel kept up his massaging. "What else?"

"Disturbing phone calls, and I have copies of notes she has received. All of them are the same. They want her to die. Then there were errant prescriptions sent to her, and her pharmacist knew nothing about it. Her own attorney has recommended putting the house up for sale and moving to a much more manageable abode."

Daniel chuckled. "An abode? I'd look at the attorney."

"She's had him in her employ for over three decades. He was her husband's legal representation for his business."

"Is she his sole client?"

"I don't know, Daniel."

"Then, I'd begin there. Wait, why am I telling you to do something about this? You aren't a professional. You aren't a detective."

"But, I am good at gathering information, and she trusts me."

"What else do you have so I can have that pie?"

Gretchen sighed deeply. "I have her list of suspects, some other documents, and my own photos. She changed her will last year, knocking off her son and grandson."

"That'll make people want you dead. Who gets everything?"

"I don't know. I would imagine her recently found great-granddaughter will be the heir."

Daniel patted her leg. "Is she capable of planning the demise of her great-grandmother?"

Gretchen's laughter filled the room. "She's a little girl, and she doesn't have an evil bone in her body."

"What about her parents?"

"Her biological father is in jail...that's the evil grandson, her mother is a lovely woman who worked very hard to get out of the drug world, and her stepfather works with Devlin at the DEA."

"Oh."

"Oh, indeed, Daniel." Gretchen shifted, lifting her legs from Daniel's lap. "I'm getting that pie and more coffee. I'll allow you to look over the papers Mrs. Notte gave me and my photos."

"Allow?" Daniel murmured.

Gretchen looked back. "Did you say something?"

"No, dear. I'd be happy to look at your evidence."

"And suspects," Gretchen added. "Of course, the list is expansive. There're other family members who just might be involved…"

Daniel dropped his head back onto the top of the couch. "Oh Lord, here we go again." He thought he'd lowered his voice enough to not be heard, but the voice from the kitchen dispelled that thought.

"Do you want that pie or not, Daniel?"

"Yes, dear."

Chapter Four

"Then look at this note." Gretchen pushed the piece of paper across the island toward the professional investigator. He took a quick sip of coffee after his bite of chocolate cream pie. The detective in him was more interested in the actual bullet hole in a window that was yards away from the street in front of the house.

"How long has this been going on?"

Gretchen shook her head. "I'm not sure. I'll have to ask more questions, but I will tell you that her butler slash personal assistant is very worried. There was a mistaken prescription–"

"That can happen," Daniel muttered as he scanned the list of suspects. "G, she's listed a former flame from high school. Is this gentleman even alive?"

"I've counted out a few, including the gentleman who delivers her newspaper. He can't possibly have a motive."

Daniel glanced up. "You think? This is silly. Someone is just playing a prank on a poor old woman."

Gretchen sniffed. "A lovely old rich woman. She is a very, very rich woman who has disowned her drug-dealing grandson, and her criminal son. She changed that will, and I bet that's when all of this began. The main suspect should be the attorney, but why would he care? Did he stand to inherit?"

"Maybe. You said he was her husband's corporate attorney. Maybe he had been promised an amount of money, and now he sees it all going to a grade schoolgirl who just entered an old lady's life. It could be the attorney." *Then again, what if the associates of her son and grandson decided to send a message by harassing Mrs. Notte?*

Gretchen placed the remainder of the pie into the refrigerator and poured another cup of coffee. She didn't care about the caffeine. She'd be up late enough making notes about each suspect. *I need Lily and her whiteboard and maybe some of those multi-colored post-it notes.*

"Daniel, who else could it be?"

Instead of answering, Daniel brought his plate and cup over to the sink. "Someone who knows that will has been changed and may not be very happy about it. Someone who sees a vulnerable wealthy advanced-aged woman with a medical condition or two and wants to get their share before she dies. It may even be someone who gets off by just creating chaos. And you're sure about the butler?"

Gretchen walked into Daniel's arms. "Silly, it's not always the butler."

"But it could be?"

"No, absolutely not. He is loyal to a fault."

"Then maybe it's someone he knows who doesn't want to wait any longer to share whatever he is going to receive." Daniel kissed her soundly on the lips. "If he's as close to Mrs. Notte as you say he is, he would be easily manipulated after her death. I have to get up early tomorrow. Let's go to bed."

"What you're telling me is I need to see that will to really gain insight into who all the players are?"

Daniel rubbed his chin in thought. "I'm not sure I said that, but that's a great start. I thought I said, let's go to bed. I missed you today."

Gretchen pulled out of his embrace and patted his back as she passed. "You miss me every day, as well you should."

"Does that mean you're heading into the bedroom?" Daniel asked hopefully.

"Maybe. I was actually going to the shower."

Daniel followed quickly behind. "I like it when you go to the shower."

Surprisingly, Gretchen giggled as if she was a teenager again. She'd never giggled even when she was younger, but it seemed this man made her feel giddy, joyful. "And you like it when you join me."

"Yes, ma'am." Daniel knew the word rankled her.

"And what did I tell you about that word?" Gretchen asked sternly as she stopped in her tracks. Daniel nearly ran into her.

"Never say it. Are we still–"

Gretchen grabbed his hand. "Come on. I missed you too."

It was midnight, and Gretchen remained awake. Daniel drifted off to sleep a couple of hours ago, but not her, despite a shower session which concluded under the sheets. She reached out and patted his leg.

His breathing was slow and steady, but as soon as she touched him, he moved. "What?"

"Nothing. I'm just thinking."

Daniel turned and placed a protective arm across her body. "Think about it tomorrow. You are a good woman to help your friend. I won't wake you in the morning." He kissed her cheek and closed his eyes again. *He'd call Devlin Pierce first thing to see if his idea about the drug dealers could possibly be true.*

A good woman? I've never been accused of that before. I'm not sure I like that. I've always been the eccentric, the glamorous, the obnoxious, the elite Gretchen Malloy, premier event and wedding planner. And now I'm good? Yuk.

Everyone always said Lily was nice. Gretchen contended she was just being nice to her client, but no, the woman was genuinely nice. Yet, Gretchen considered Lily Schmidt Pierce her bestie. Had the niceness been rubbing off on her? Could she be content being a good woman?

Gretchen casually looked over at the man sleeping next to her. Detective Daniel Williams had been such an unexpected pleasure, in more ways than she could count. He was so honest. If he thought she was good, then it must be so, but Gretchen Malloy had a few good days of obnoxious behavior in her, and she'd begin acting out again tomorrow. Mrs. Notte needed her.

Chapter Five

"Thank you so much for meeting with me." Gretchen walked quickly into the attorney's office on The Plaza. She looked around the room and noticed several expensive replica sculptures, including one of a cowboy on a horse.

Last week, Mrs. Notte had scheduled the appointment with William Gilliard, her corporate and family attorney for decades. She was delighted that Gretchen Malloy "was on the case".

The older lawyer showed Gretchen to the chair in front of his desk and had his assistant bring in two coffees. As the assistant left, Gretchen noticed the eye contact between the employer and employee. *And what is going on there?*

"Mrs. Notte said to meet with you, and when the dear lady says to meet with someone, I do. I believe my wife used your business for our anniversary party two years ago."

"Yes, Mr. Gilliard, I did plan the event. Your wife was a sheer delight to work for."

"Yes, she was very pleased with all of your work. Now, what can I do for you, Ms. Malloy?"

"Mrs. Notte has informed you that she believes someone is threatening her life?"

Mr. Gilliard nodded. The pen in his left hand drummed on the desk. "Yes, she has. Oh, and she said to give you a copy of her will. It will be on my assistant's desk. You can pick it up on your way out."

"Thank you. I'm just doing some leg work. I also have a detective looking into the threats." The lawyer across from her only nodded. *He doesn't need to know my detective is sleeping next to me, does he?*

"I'm very concerned for her well-being. I've known her for so long, and I'd feel awful if something happened to her."

Now Gretchen was the one who nodded. "Mr. Gilliard, do you have any idea who might want to prank or scare her in this manner? Was anyone aced out of her will when it was altered?"

"Maybe a charity or two. She wanted to make sure that Angelica had funding for her education, a stipend for her parents' expenses so that they could improve their lifestyle and assure that the young lady would have funding for the future no matter what she decided to do with her life. I have included a copy of the old will in your packet so you can compare."

"That is wonderful. Thank you. So, who could possibly be doing this?"

Mr. Gilliard finally adjusted his position. He leaned forward and placed his pen on the desk. "I would think the butler?" He then grinned.

"Everyone always thinks that, but the man is devoted to her."

"Then I'd say her ungrateful son and grandson, but they're both in federal prisons."

Gretchen nodded. "It might be retribution for their debts, but she disowned them completely. This seems to be different, perhaps a personal threat?"

"I don't know of anyone who might feel slighted by Mrs. Notte, do you?"

Gretchen smiled. "That's why I asked you. Thank you for your time and cooperation. I'll inform Mrs. Notte that you were very forthcoming." The elite planner didn't know if that was appropriate to say, but she'd heard it said on numerous detective television programs. She stood up, shook the man's hand, and was shuttled out of the office. She stopped in front of the assistant's desk.

Gretchen glanced at the name plaque. "Diana, Mr. Gilliard had a packet for me?"

"Oh yes, Ms. Malloy." The woman whose glasses set on the edge of her nose, reached back and grabbed a thick manila envelope. "I have copies of Mrs. Notte's old and new wills, and trust and foundation documents. If you need anything else, please let us know."

As Gretchen took the information, she peered inside. Thankfully, since it was January, Gretchen wasn't that busy with work. Just reading all of this mess was going to take hours. "I will. Thank you."

Gretchen grabbed her coat and opened the office door, but as she turned to leave, Diana stood at her side. "Ms. Malloy, you need to know something."

The assistant whispered, and Gretchen knew something was up. "Yes?"

"There was a man here last fall who was inquiring about Mrs. Notte. He said he was with an insurance company, but I didn't believe him. I don't know what he and Mr. Gilliard discussed, but it just seemed off. Does that make sense?"

"Indeed, it does. Could I have his name?"

Diana nodded and headed to her desk. She looked at her computer screen for a few minutes and wrote down a name and phone number on a notepad. Handing it to Gretchen, Diana added a small envelope under the note. "Mrs. Notte can be difficult, but no one deserves to be afraid. I hope you can help her."

Gretchen stuffed the items into her coat pocket. "Thank you, and I hope I can help her too."

Once she reached the car, Gretchen called Daniel.

"Detective Williams."

"Detective, I have two copies of wills and enough information to read for days. Are you working this weekend?"

Gretchen heard the background noise of the police department. "I have this feeling I'm working for you, darling."

"That's the answer I wanted to hear. Then, there's an insurance man who came to the lawyer last year. This just keeps getting better and better."

Daniel cleared his throat. "Or worse and worse depending on your perspective. The police won't touch this?"

"They didn't. Do you want to ask someone down there?"

"I have reached out to a friend. It doesn't seem that any of this involves her son or grandson and their business associates, but you never know."

"But you will ask around, Daniel?"

"I will, but I don't want you in danger," Daniel answered. "Gretchen, don't get yourself into trouble."

"You are a very sweet man," Gretchen purred. "I'll see you tonight, won't I?"

"Yes. Are you cooking again?"

"No, we're back to take out."

"Then I'll pick up Chinese. See you around six."

What a good man he is! "I'm heading home right now to begin my reading. Oh, and don't forget we have a charity event Saturday night at the Convention Center. Make sure you have your tux ready."

"Yes, ma–Gretchen. I've got to go."

You saved yourself a lot of grief, Daniel! Gretchen looked over at the packet in her passenger seat. She couldn't wait to wade through all of the information, but first she had to do a bit of work on two upcoming events. Gretchen prided herself on her work ethic, but those two wills seemed to be screaming at her. *Read me!*

Once in her apartment, Gretchen changed into her standard winter uniform of a heavy sweater and leggings. She put the coffee on and headed for her laptop. The wedding season would be a busy one for her. She had five rather large events for several of the most famous families in the city. But she was looking forward to Saturday's charity party which was planned by the children's hospital.

She never missed the night, and she always wore a bright red gown with red designer heels. This year would be no exception, but she'd be on the arm of a rather attractive Daniel Williams. His custom-made tuxedo made him look as though he was worth a million bucks.

"But I know you're worth way more than that, dear Daniel." Last year, after she was no longer a suspect in his murder investigation, Daniel and she had begun slowly. She thought he was just a lowly member of the KCPD. Of course, she'd researched him online but always hit walls. All she had managed to discover was he was divorced, and he used to be a financial wizard in New York City. His ex was in fashion and had moved to Paris to make her mark.

Only a couple of weeks ago he'd surprised her with a private plane trip with him at the helm. Dear Daniel took her to his family's private island in the Bahamas. He was full of surprises. One after the other enchanted her. The man was making her feel flutters and tremors that none other had, except for Chance.

"But you left me twice," she said out loud. She poured her coffee and sat down at her corner desk to begin answering several emails. Those wills kept yelling.

It was almost four in the afternoon by the time she grabbed a snack of cheese and apple slices and settled on the couch with the two copies. She also noticed other documents on Mrs. Notte's trust. Gretchen began with the newest last will and testament.

It was as she had suspected. Angelica was receiving the lion's share of the wealth. Mrs. Notte's trusted assistant was given a lifetime income and was named as the caretaker of a beach house in Florida. Her son and grandson had been completely thrown off of any inheritance except for the one dollar each was to receive. The mansion would be sold, and the beach house was to be given to...

"Lily!" *What in the world? My bestie is inheriting Mrs. Notte's beach house? Why wouldn't Angelica receive that too? They live in Florida. They could visit–*

"Oh, Mrs. Notte's is counting on Lily's good nature." There was a stipulation that if Lily wanted to relieve herself of that responsibility at any time, the ownership would revert to Mrs. Notte's sole heir, little Angelica when she turned twenty-five years of age. Mrs. Notte's attorney even added that Lily's stewardship and ownership was always to welcome Angelica and her family, and that her trusted Barrett would live the remainder of his life there if he wished.

Gretchen paused. Her eyes looked over her eyeglasses at the cell phone on the table in front of her. *Lily will be so surprised, but I can't tell her. Mrs. Notte is counting on me and my discretion.* "No, I can't tell her. I need to read more."

The remainder of the document covered legal matters and more trust information. There were smaller amounts of money left to a few family members, but none of the allowance was more than fifty thousand dollars. Her sister-in-law, who was now in her eighties as well, was left one hundred thousand. There were two great nieces and two nieces given twenty thousand each. She even provided a favorite piece of art and ten thousand dollars to her former daughter-in-law who lived on a ranch in Montana with her current husband.

There was also a tongue-lashing for her son Bernard and her grandson Garrett. How could they ruin the family name? Why had they gone into the drug business? How could he have stolen her art? Why did they steal her favorite necklace?

"A necklace? When did they do that?" Lily had told her of the antics of the two Notte men who dabbled in drugs, embezzlement, murder, and art forgery. Dev and his friends had taken the two men down, but Lily had been placed in terrible danger throughout the adventure.

By the time Gretchen was reading codicils and the revocable trust, her eyes were tired and her stomach growled. Mrs. Notte and her attorney had created document after document that were sound and hopefully unbreakable. The woman might be fearful about her future, but she was shrewd. Mrs. Notte wasn't a fool, and apparently never had been. Her husband had left her a good amount of money, but he had also fiddled away vast sums. She built back their fortune with investments and enlightened business deals.

"What a woman! She's a lot like me." Gretchen removed her glasses and rubbed her eyes. She squinted to see the kitchen clock. Daniel would be here soon with food, and she'd have so many questions for him.

Chapter Six

"Can you check for a police report that would've been filed on that necklace?"

Daniel opened the trash bin and slid the boxes from dinner within. "When did it happen?"

"I don't know. Can't you do your police thing and find it? How many Mrs. Nottes can there be in this city? I only know of one," Gretchen said, seemingly annoyed at his lack of attention to her inquisition.

"Honey, I'll do what I can."

"Could you do it now?"

Daniel shoved the bin back into the cabinet. "No, I cannot."

"Daniel, you're being very difficult." Gretchen almost stomped out of the kitchen and took her place in the corner of the couch. She pretended to look over more papers.

"I've had a crappy day. Thank you for asking," Daniel yelled. He opened the refrigerator and grabbed a bottle of his favorite beer. He took two drinks before he turned back around to see the woman in the living room.

"Not every day can be perfect," Gretchen murmured.

Daniel took his place in the chair across from her. "Says the woman who gets something in her brain and won't let go of it until the entire world stops."

Gretchen removed her glasses and bit on the edge of one of the arms. "Are you insinuating that I only think of myself?"

"I'd never say that," Daniel said quietly. "I'd say that you consume yourself with things that aren't your business. Yes, I'd say you do many things for your own self-interest. That's who you are. You love the limelight and to be needed in any way."

Gretchen's eyes became tiny slits. "Now you're insinuating that I'm needy?"

"Not insinuating. I'm saying it."

"How dare you?"

Daniel actually smiled. "Not once tonight have you talked about anything but this necklace, the will, Mrs. Notte…You haven't asked about my day. It's not that I want to talk about what happened today, but dang it, you are like a dog with a bone, and–"

"Go on," Gretchen suggested as she folded her arms over her ample breasts.

"This isn't any of your damn business. You aren't a professional investigator, you're a–"

Gretchen stood up. "What am I, Daniel?"

"You're a damn event planner!" He stood up and stared at her. They were within inches of each other. This was a duel to the death.

"You are wrong, Detective Williams. I'm the elite planner of this city! I'm just not a damn one; I'm the best."

Gretchen slid past his body and walked into the bedroom, slamming the door behind her. She sat down on her bed and waited. She watched the clock on the side table where Daniel usually left his wristwatch. One minute, two minutes, three minutes…

"Why isn't he coming in?"

Then she heard the front door shut. She looked at the clock again. Five minutes…ten minutes. "Fine. I'll be the bigger person."

She opened the bedroom door dramatically. "We should talk about–" The living room was empty as was the kitchen. Daniel's overcoat was gone as was his jacket and tie. She looked down and his shoes were absent from where he always left them when he came home.

"He left me? Me?" *I'm the one who walks away. I won't allow a man to leave me again.*

And the fearless elite planner of the city of fountains began to cry. Her mascara ran down her face, and her nose became congested. "I don't cry over men!"

Gretchen blew her nose and cleaned her face with a tissue. "Until now. When did this happen? Daniel!"

She grabbed her phone and began a search. She found the name and hit the number. "Jerry, hello this is Gretchen Malloy. I'm Daniel's friend, I mean Detective Williams' friend."

The detective on the other end of the line was taken back. "Yes, Ms. Malloy. What can I do for you?"

"Well, I know this is an unusual request, but could you possibly tell me what happened today? Daniel just wasn't himself, and I thought you might know–"

"It was a bad day. If you watch the news, you'll see the story. There was a shooting, and two children were killed. The mother was inconsolable and tried to harm herself on the scene. Daniel fought with her and grabbed the knife before we had another fatality."

Gretchen gulped. *That's absolutely awful.* "Oh," she answered. What more was there to say? "Thank you. I understand. I'm sorry for all of you, and for that dear woman. I appreciate you telling me."

"Is he okay?"

"No, he isn't. Maybe you could call him, please?" Gretchen collapsed onto the couch and hid her face with a pillow. When had she last said please?

"Of course. Thanks for the heads up."

"No, thank you for all you do. Goodnight."

Before the man could say anything more to make her feel worse than she already did, Gretchen ended the call. She hit another button.

"Gretchen, can I call you back? Dev and I are trying to get Andrew to sleep and Emi is being–" Lily Pierce heard sobbing on the other side of the call. "Gretchen, what is it? Are you okay?"

"I'm selfish and needy. I don't think of anyone but myself unless it brings me fame or attention. I'm an awful person."

Lily had no words. *Is she drunk? What has happened?*

There's no way Gretchen went to a revival and has been reborn, is there?

"And he said he loves me, and I can't say it back now. I'm a terrible person, but I'm still the best planner in this region, and definitely in this city."

And she's back! "Take your daughter. I have to talk to Gretchen." Lily handed off her infant and headed into the bedroom for privacy. "Gretchen, I'm here. Daniel loves you?"

"Not anymore because I'm an awful person."

Lily rolled her eyes. "What happened? What did you do or not do?"

"I don't think of others."

Lily thought about her next words carefully. "Well, you're a busy woman, but you can be kind. You love my children, and you perform miracles for your clients."

"Your children are the only ones I have in my life, and my clients pay me for my services. Oh Lord, I'm a call girl!"

"You are not a call girl," Lily said sternly. "Stop being a drama queen and concisely tell me what has happened. I don't have time–" Lily watched as her naked son ran away from his father. Dev ran by next, his wet shirt clinging to his chest. He was holding his newborn like a small football. "Just tell me."

"So, I'm helping Mrs. Notte, and I'm consumed by this case. Daniel had a bad day. Two small children were killed, and he prevented the mother from harming herself, and I didn't care about him. I didn't notice he was upset.

He hardly said anything during dinner. I'm an awful person."

"Awful? No, I wouldn't say that exactly. You can be absolutely the most generous woman I know, and then–"

"I can be an ass."

Lily smiled. "There is that. Yes, you can be. Daniel said he loved you?"

"Yes, and I left. I didn't say anything back. We've said we love each other, but this was somehow different. He really meant it."

"Do you love him?"

There was a pause in the conversation. Gretchen's crying ceased. "I don't know. The only man I've ever loved was Chance and look where that got me."

"You tell me that your life has been amazing. You're the great Gretchen Malloy," Lily said, hoping to comfort her friend. "There's no one else like you. You're uniquely you."

"I am. I know, but I've made a mess this time. Can you come home?"

"I am home. Here."

"You know what I mean. Come here, to Kansas City. You can fix it. I know you can."

"Are we talking about fixing Daniel and you?"

"That too," Gretchen admitted. "I know Mrs. Notte would love to see you."

"Gretchen, **you** need to fix this with the detective. You need to do it now if he's who you want."

Lily listened for a response but there was silence. Finally, Gretchen cleared her throat. "What if I can't? What if the great Gretchen Malloy has completely messed up this time?"

"The Gretchen Malloy I know can do anything and in six-inch heels. Go get him," Lily directed.

"I'll call you tomorrow, bestie!"

Lily sat on the edge of the bed and wondered what was really going on with her "bestie". Dev returned to the room, holding a pajama clad small boy in one arm and his baby girl in the other.

"What did the stiletto terrorist want?"

"Guidance, I think." Lily gathered her son in her arms, kissing him on the forehead. "Your Auntie G has a problem."

Dev chuckled. "What is her problem now?"

"It's a man."

Dev switched children with his wife. "Of course. Isn't it always with her? Don't tell me the detective is still involved."

"It's more than that," Lily admitted. "He loves her."

Dev shook his head. "I'm taking this one to his bed, and little man and I will pray for Daniel. He called me, but we didn't discuss Gretchen."

Lily eyed her husband suspiciously. "About what?"

"The Notte men. Mrs. Notte is being harassed?"

"Yes. You do not think some of their connections could be the masterminds, do you?"

Dev shook his head as his son's finger tried to enter his mouth. "Nah. Garrett and Bernard were the heads of their operations. Anyone they were associated with is long gone or has already received their dollars from them."

"Well, it has to be someone. Maybe someone didn't get paid?"

Dev leaned down and kissed his wife on the cheek. "Explain one thing to me. How can the detective possibly love Gretchen Malloy?"

Before Lily could answer, her husband had turned and was headed down the hallway to Andrew's room. She looked down at her daughter, still asleep after all of tonight's action. "It's easy when you really know her."

Chapter Seven

Daniel didn't answer his phone the next morning, but Gretchen received a text. It was brief, telling her the necklace report was from two years ago. However, only three months later, Mrs. Notte's assistant informed the police it had been found, misplaced by a relative of the family.

Gretchen stared at the screensaver on her phone. It was a lovely photo of Daniel and her at Christmas. They had stopped on the streets of The Plaza and taken a selfie near one of the brightly lit towers of one of the buildings. Her finger traced his face. "Daniel, how am I going to fix this?"

She had a consultation at noon for a wedding later in the year. One of the planners for the bride was pregnant and wouldn't be able to fulfill her contract. The mother remembered Gretchen from a board they served on together. Gretchen would see if they would be a good fit, and if she was content to step in as a replacement.

After nearly an hour of quiet contemplation, thirty sit ups, a plank or two, and thirty minutes of yoga, Gretchen sent an email to Daniel's private account. She explained how sorry she was; that she was thoughtless and only thinking of herself. She thanked him for the information, and she admitted one more thing.

"Daniel, I was very familiar with how Isaac felt when he ran away. He wanted so much more and thought his family's love was holding him back. I explained to him that once I did the same thing. I wanted the life I have. I have a lovely home, an expensive car, exquisite clothing and jewelry, and I am well connected. There was a time when I wanted love, but Chance made decisions without consulting me. He told me he loved me, but he didn't treat me as if he did. He did the same thing when he jumped back into my life when I met you.

What I never have said is that when Chance joined the Marines, I ran away. I graduated, had my bags packed, and drove as far as I could in the opposite direction. I didn't allow him to contact me again. He found me through letters to my parents and Amy years later, but I couldn't be hurt again.

You said you loved me. I hope you still do. I won't run away this time. I promise. Please forgive me."

Gretchen hit send and closed her eyes in a prayer. Almost immediately there was an answer from her detective. *"What do you want for dinner?"*

Gretchen smiled. *I won't run, and he's apparently staying. This might work.*

After the noon meeting, and the signing of a contract for her services for one of the weddings of the year, Gretchen swung by Mrs. Notte's home. She was welcomed by the octogenarian.

Mrs. Notte looked around past Gretchen and pulled on her arm. "Get in here. It's not safe out there."

"What is going on?" Gretchen kept her coat on as she followed the woman into the darkened office.

"I've had another threat. Poor Barrett was nearly killed on the street right outside. He was getting the mail, and a car came up on the sidewalk and nearly took the poor man out. He has a few bruises and cuts, but he's alive. It was that same red car."

"Call the police," Gretchen instructed.

"No, I'm fine," the trusted assistant said as he joined the ladies. "I'm sure they meant no harm."

Gretchen was perplexed, but she remained calm. This was a time she needed to act like she was at a wedding, and the cake hadn't arrived yet. When the bride asked if it was lovely, Gretchen would smile and walk away. "It'll be exactly what you want." She'd calmly walk away until she was out of sight and then run like crazy, calling the shop, and formulating a plan for a backup cake. Never allow them to see you sweat. *Or in my case, glisten!*

As Mrs. Notte sat down in her chair, Gretchen took her position on the opposite side of the desk. "You both know who it is, don't you?"

"She's just angry," Mrs. Notte lamented.

"Who is just angry?"

Barrett patted his boss's hand. "You need to tell Ms. Malloy."

The elderly woman leaned back in her chair, closing her eyes and then opening them slowly in defeat. "It's one of my great nieces. I threw her out after I returned from Florida last year. I noticed some items missing, and I confronted her."

"Was she involved in the necklace theft two years ago?" Gretchen's question seemed to surprise the other two in the room.

"She brought it back. It was all my grandson Garrett's fault. He needed money for his defense, and dear Lolly needed her drugs and a new life. Garrett introduced those nasty substances into her life. When her own mother told her to get clean or move out, she chose to come to Kansas City. She soon ran out of money and showed up on my doorstep. Little did I know that my grandson had put her up to it. He told her about the necklace. He knew a fence. My, I've learned a lot of criminal terminology in the last few years."

"But she brought it back?"

Mrs. Notte nodded. "Two months later she returned it. She had second thoughts, and she said she missed me. I allowed her back into my house. Nothing else happened. She was delightful company, when she was here. She would go missing for weeks on end. Last year, she came by the house while we were in Florida. My caretaker allowed her in to gather her things from the room she was using. She was leaving town, and he didn't think anything of it. That's when I was missing several items that she probably received pennies on the dollar for."

Gretchen's brain was working overtime. "Could I please see the necklace?"

"The one she returned? Why does that matter?"

"Mrs. Notte, I just want to check it out."

Barrett was directed to return with the piece of jewelry, and when he did, he handed it directly to Gretchen.

The ever-prepared planner pulled out a jeweler's loop from her purse and began to examine the piece. It was a heavy, elaborate necklace of diamonds and deep blue sapphires. Its weight seemed correct, but upon further examination, Gretchen noticed something amiss.

"Mrs. Notte, have you had a jeweler look at this since it was returned?"

"Of course not. She returned it. The insurance company was happy they didn't have to pay out a claim."

Gretchen looked over the piece one more time. "I have a friend who knows jewels very well. I'd like him to look this over, but I personally think that this is a fake. It's well made, but it's all glass, and a machine made it. You can tell that no artisan touched this."

Mrs. Notte sat up straight in her chair. "Are you sure?"

"Almost. Maybe there's a few genuine stones, but I doubt it. The frame is definitely machine made."

"Could you have your friend come here?"

Gretchen thought about her friend. *Will Daniel do this for me?* "I can check."

Mrs. Notte fluttered her hand. "Do it. Do it now. I need to know."

Gretchen called Daniel. In two rings he actually answered. "Yes?"

"I'm sorry to bother you, but I need your help." Gretchen would've preferred to say she just needed him, but she would say it later privately.

"I realize you aren't going to let this go. What can I do?"

"I'm at Mrs. Notte's home, and I believe you should see this piece of jewelry. It is the necklace involved in the theft from two years ago."

On the other end of the phone, Daniel continued to drive. He was only minutes away. "Text me the address, and I'll be there in a few minutes."

"I'm doing it now. You'll actually be here in a few?"

"Yes. See you in a bit."

Well, that went fine. Fine isn't the best, but at least he's coming. "He'll be here in just a few minutes," Gretchen reported to Mrs. Notte.

In less than five minutes, Daniel walked through the foyer and into the office of the large mansion. Gretchen stood immediately to introduce Mrs. Notte.

Detective Williams was the perfect gentleman. He greeted the elderly woman and informed her that he was a homicide detective, but his family owned one of the premier diamond and precious jewel companies in the world. After a little conversation, Mrs. Notte realized that her husband had sat on a board years ago with Daniel's grandfather. Gretchen noticed the woman trusted Daniel almost immediately.

"And here's the necklace and my loop." Gretchen handed over both items to Daniel who now sat in a chair next to her.

"Mrs. Notte, what had the necklace been appraised at, and when was it last done by the insurance company?"

Daniel began to examine the piece. "I had all of my jewelry appraised and insured five years ago when my son and grandson began acting shifty."

Daniel looked up and removed the loop from his eye. He and Gretchen shared a smile. "Shifty, I see."

Mrs. Notte pointed at the piece in Daniel's hand. "That very piece was appraised at over one quarter of a million dollars. It is the most expensive piece I own."

Daniel grimaced. "Well, I'm sorry to say that this is a manufactured piece and it was done fairly recently, possibly when it was supposedly stolen a few years back. It's glass and machine made. Maybe, maybe it's worth three hundred dollars. It's a good costume piece."

Mrs. Notte fell back in her chair. "My niece did that, didn't she?"

Daniel's confusion showed on his face. Gretchen patted his arm. "Lolly, her great niece was possibly in league with the drug dealer grandson Garrett. She took the necklace. She returned it a few months later."

"So, they had a fake made. That was all prepared in advance by Garrett?"

Gretchen nodded. "That's my suspicion."

"Where's your great niece now?" Daniel asked as he passed the necklace to the man whom he assumed was the butler.

"I have no idea."

Barrett cleared his throat. "She's been watching the house. She nearly hit me with a car today."

Daniel pulled out a pad and began writing. "Can you give me a description, the car, make, plate number?"

Barrett saw how distressed his mistress was and motioned with his head into the hallway. "Perhaps we could speak in the kitchen. Ms. Malloy, would you like a coffee or hot tea? Madame?"

Mrs. Notte nodded affirmatively. Gretchen agreed to a hot tea. Daniel followed the other man out of the room.

"Is that your detective?" Mrs. Notte asked as soon as they were alone. "Lily told me about him. Devlin likes him."

"Ah, well, I hope he is mine. I was very foolish last night and made a huge mistake," Gretchen lamented sadly.

"He loves you, you know. I can tell."

Gretchen managed a slight smile. "I hope he does. There're times when I'm very unlovable."

"Nonsense," Mrs. Notte said, raising her voice slightly. "A strong man will always want a strong woman. You are, and he most definitely is. He has a finesse."

"He has a particular charm, among other fine attributes."

Mrs. Notte winked. "I remember fine attributes fondly. Hours in bed on a rainy afternoon, right?"

Gretchen nearly blushed despite her age. But there wasn't anything she had or hadn't done that could embarrass herself. She had fond memories of one day like that, but she had more recollections of nights in his arms. But, surely Daniel and she were just passing in the night? He was younger. Wouldn't he want a family? He said he didn't need that in their relationship, but still Gretchen wondered.

When the two men returned, the discussion turned toward Lolly. Daniel already had a lead on the car. It was parked in a hamburger restaurant lot right off The Plaza. "I'm having her brought over here right now. We will have a little talk."

The group moved to the larger sitting room on the other side of the house. Daniel took a quick look at several of Mrs. Notte's other pieces of high value jewelry in her safe. Thankfully, every item was genuine, but he recommended she have her favorite jeweler take a look just to make sure.

Finally, two policemen led the young woman into the room. Daniel had a few private words with the officers and released them. When he returned to the group, everyone was silent, including Mrs. Notte who just looked at her great niece.

"Ms. Lolly Tatum, could I see your driver's license, please? I'm Detective Williams, and you're here to discuss a certain piece of jewelry."

The young woman searched through her purse and almost threw the license at the man.

Finally, Mrs. Notte voiced her opinion. "You are better than that. The man is a detective. You have some manners, young lady."

"I don't know why I'm here," she spat out. "You can't keep me."

Before anyone could contradict her, Daniel answered. "You're right, but I can take you with me to headquarters.

Ms. Tatum, your license is expired, and you're driving a car that has expired plates. It's registered to your parents. We should call them and make sure you have permission to have it here in the city."

Lolly shook her head and laughed. "This is just great. I'm just trying to have a life."

"As what exactly?" Mrs. Notte asked. "You took my necklace, then you brought it back, but it's a fake. What did you do with the real one?"

"I think you've lost your marbles, old lady."

Barrett nearly lunged at the young woman, Mrs. Notte responded quickly. "I have not, and I heard you that day. You were sorry. You ran away because you were afraid. No, you ran away to sell that necklace off for money, for drugs. How could you? Lolly, when you showed up at my doorstep, I took you in despite the fact you'd run away from your parents, from your job, and your life."

"You can't prove anything."

Daniel handed the license back. He grimaced and knelt down in front of Lolly. "Look, I actually can prove that. It only took me twenty minutes while I drank coffee to find the fence, to realize Garrett and you have had contact while he's been in prison, and to know that he told you where to go to have the necklace replicated. What I need to know now is if you've been threatening and harassing your great aunt?"

"Do you think I'd tell you either way? You already have your opinion of me."

Daniel stood up. "Actually, I don't. They may, and they have every right to think the worst of you. I think you're in over your head. I think you need someone like me to get you out of the hole you've dug for yourself. Am I even close?"

"Why would I need you?"

Daniel shrugged. "Because, if you think that Garrett is going to allow you to keep all that money, you're the one who has lost their marbles. He's ruthless. His father is ruthless, and you've been stealing items out of this house for them, but then you got greedy. Trust me, just because they're in prison doesn't mean they can't touch you. You need me."

Gretchen felt pride. Actually, she felt relieved. This was her detective, and for once he wasn't interrogating her. This girl certainly was in over her head.

Lolly turned away and began to study a family photo on the mantle.

Daniel looked over at Gretchen. This girl had no idea what trouble she was in, and an expired driver's license was the least of her worries. "Lolly, did you shoot through the window?"

She didn't answer. Daniel continued. "Lolly, did you use your old key to gain entrance through the garden doors? Did you take those items last year? I'll have a list of them before the end of tonight if you've forgotten. Did you trade those prescriptions in order to murder your great aunt?"

Finally, Lolly turned her head. "What are you talking about? I'd never hurt her. I'd steal from her, but never–"

"I see," Daniel said slowly. "So, there's something else going on here besides a confused and desperate young woman who doesn't have a damn clue that she's terribly inadequate to play with the big boys. They will hurt you, Lolly. I can assure you of that."

"So now what?" She remained defiant despite Daniel's best efforts.

Daniel shoved her license into his pocket and pulled out his car keys. "You and I are going down to my office, we're going to talk a bit, and then you'll be placed in a holding cell for further questioning. You may even be charged for theft, conspiracy, and–"

"Gaslighting? Can that be a charge?" Gretchen asked. Lolly looked beyond the detective in her sight way to see the woman with the high heels.

"Who are you?" Lolly almost spat out the question.

"I'm Gretchen Malloy, and I'm investigating on behalf of Mrs. Notte."

Lolly scoffed at the declaration. "Seriously? You look more like some retired beauty queen."

"Thank you," Gretchen answered smugly. She took the description as a compliment.

Daniel turned away briefly to smile. There was one thing about Gretchen Malloy, she never denied being herself. "Ms. Tatum, we need to go."

"What about my car?"

"Your parents' car will be here for them to pick up." Mrs. Notte stood, her cane tapping on the rug. "I'll update them on what is going on."

As Daniel took Lolly by the arm, he motioned for

Mrs. Notte's butler. They shared a few words. Daniel turned around and nodded at Gretchen before leaving.

Mrs. Notte collapsed onto her sofa and heaved a dramatic sigh. "Why? Why on earth is my family so, so–"

"Criminal? Messed up? Corrupt? How am I doing?" Gretchen asked.

Mrs. Notte surprisingly broke out into a generous laugh. "My, you do have a way with words. Yes, my family is something else. I'm not sure what yet, but they are something."

"All families have something. You should see them on a wedding day. I have so many stories I could tell you," Gretchen acknowledged.

"Barrett, could you get Ms. Malloy and I one of the good bottles of wine?"

"But Madame, you know you shouldn't."

"Yet, I will. Please, and grab a glass for yourself as well."

The devoted employee smiled and bowed. "Yes, Mrs. Notte. I do think we all need a drink."

"And, if she has time, Ms. Malloy will regale us with some wonderful stories that will make me feel better."

Gretchen understood completely. "I do have some goodies, and you'll know a few of the families from the club."

Mrs. Notte clapped. "I love good gossip, and I especially enjoy good company."

Gretchen had given up on Daniel for the night. After a couple of glasses of the best cabernet she'd ever tasted, and after a lovely mix of appetizers, Gretchen arrived home. *Why is my lovely, quiet home now dreary and lonely?* She knew the answer, and that answer had a name… Daniel.

She was reading in bed when she finally received a phone call. It was nearly ten. "Hello?"

"Gretchen, I'm sorry I didn't get back to you."

"No, I'm sorry, Daniel. My behavior–"

"It's fine. I understand."

"No, I don't think you do. I was–"

"Stop," Daniel interrupted. "It's been a long day, hell, it's been a long week, and its only Tuesday. We can talk this weekend. We are holding Lolly. She has a few more problems than just what she did to Mrs. Notte and her butler. I wanted to warn you that I'm contacting Dev Pierce. I need more info on Mrs. Notte's grandson and son."

"Well, Dev will know, and I'm sure he'll be happy to help. Daniel, you need to know I'm convinced that there is more to all of this."

Daniel knew that tone, and it usually meant Gretchen wouldn't stop until she was satisfied that Mrs. Notte would be safe, and that all was revealed. "Of course you are."

"I wouldn't be a good investigator if I just stopped now, would I?"

Daniel **should** say she wasn't an investigator, but it was useless. Gretchen had it in her head that she was a super sleuth. He had it in his head that one of these days she would get herself in big trouble or even dead if she continued to think she was like a super sleuth in stilettos. "You wouldn't be you." *That says it all, doesn't it?*

"Daniel, will you still be attending the event Saturday night with me?" As soon as Gretchen asked her question she felt like a silly schoolgirl. If he said no, she would be hurt more than when John Periwinkle ditched her at prom for that cheerleader their junior year in high school.

"Of course. The tux is ready, and I'll need a good time with my favorite lady. I'll hire a driver and car for the night."

Gretchen was beyond relieved. "Wonderful. I won't bother you then this week. I'll touch base Friday?"

"I'll try to touch base before then, but yes on Friday. Goodnight."

"Goodnight, Daniel."

He said nothing more. Perhaps Saturday night would change everything between them? Perhaps they could be who they were just a few weeks ago?

Chapter Eight

Daniel sent a car to pick up Gretchen at her apartment. He would meet her at the Convention Center. He explained he was working late, and his partner would drop him off.

"Working late my ass." Gretchen huffed and puffed and nearly blew herself off her six-inch designer heels. But when the limousine arrived, and within it was a bottle of her favorite champagne and a modest serving of crab stuffed mushrooms from her favorite restaurant, all was nearly forgiven.

Arriving alone at a large event is what Gretchen Malloy did better than anyone in the city. Before the driver opened the door she reapplied her signature red lipstick, checked her mascara one more time, and pasted a wide smile on her face. She had years of practice being alone, and she could make it look stylish so every other woman would want to do it.

She sashayed to the VIP registration desk and received her number as well as the paddle for the evening's auction. The volunteers also presented the number of her table and the rather cute Cupid lanyards that offered entry into the VIP area. Gretchen thanked the ladies for their volunteer work and headed to the nearest bar to wait for Daniel.

From her vantage point at the top of the escalator, she'd be able to see his arrival in the lobby. She smiled at guests as they landed on the second level. Gretchen managed to set up a client meeting with two ladies planning a rather large baby shower at one of the clubs. Going to events like this allowed her to see future business, and to be seen.

Gretchen finished her first glass of wine when she saw a very handsome man racing into the building. He headed directly to the reception desk, and Gretchen gathered they told him she'd already checked in. He walked briskly to the escalator and as he rode it up, he straightened his red tie that matched her dress. *He remembered.*

He stretched his neck as if the collar was strangling him and that's when he saw her. Gretchen smiled. Daniel smiled. She hoped that meant all was forgiven. He shrugged and pointed at his watch.

She heard him as he came closer. "I'm sorry. I had to—"

Gretchen kissed him suddenly. Both of her hands were filled, or she would have embraced him fiercely. But Daniel wound his arms around her back. As he pulled back, he seemed less frazzled. "I suppose that means I'm forgiven?"

Gretchen stepped back. "I should be the one saying that."

"You're not used to what I do. I usually leave the day behind, but this time I should've told you. I don't let people in. I expected you to accept my mood," he answered.

"I've been that way too for a very long time. I just threw myself into my work and had little regard for those around me. I shouldn't be so self-absorbed." *My goodness, when have I ever acknowledged my prime fault to another human being?*

Daniel bowed his head and looked up shyly at her. "Then you wouldn't be you, darling."

Gretchen handed her empty glass to her companion. "I'll allow you to get away with that if you have this refilled. I'm drinking champagne tonight."

He gave her a peck on the cheek. "Of course you are. I'll be right back. Don't move. I don't want to lose the most beautiful, glamorous woman in the room."

He could charm the pants off, well he can. How is this man in my life after all of the years? I'm not sure how this is happening, but I'm loving every minute of it. Love, there's that pesky word again.

Daniel seemed excited as he returned with her filled glass and his own bourbon. "Someone said there's a silent auction?"

"No. The last time you bid on a trip at one of these events, the entire place blew up. Literally. We had fire trucks and the ATF. I didn't mind the cute men in their gear, but I ended up looking like a mess–"

Daniel quickly offered her his arm. "Come on, G. Live a little."

"I never live a little; I live a lot, remember?"

That he did. The appetizers in the VIP area sufficed Daniel until dinner, but he was more intent on bidding on several items. "Look, it's a game at Arrowhead and you meet–"

"Yes, Daniel. You want to meet the best quarterback in the league. I could just make a call if you really want to do that."

He hurriedly marked a dollar amount and went onto the next item. "Really? Just a call. Maybe. Look at this. Look."

He's like a child in an ice cream shop. People are going to wonder about the police detective who spends thousands of dollars on charity items. But they don't know he's worth millions.

Gretchen glanced at the sheet explaining the adventure. "I'm not zip lining. If God intended me to do that, he would've given me wings."

"Oh come on. Don't be such an old–" Daniel shut his mouth quickly. "Gretchen, I didn't mean–" It was too late. A scowl had replaced her smile, and he thought he saw fire emanating from her eyes. At the least, her pupils were large.

"Old? I see. Which brings me to a very important subject."

Daniel downed the remainder of his drink. "I'm so sorry. I wanted this night to be very special since Valentine's Day is so near."

"Yes, well, Valentine's Day is highly overrated, and I'm coordinating a wedding that evening so you're off the hook. My subject we need to discuss is children."

"Children?" Daniel wasn't expecting that talking point. "What about them?"

"I can't have any." Gretchen bit her lip and waited.

"Yes, I figured that."

"Yet, you're with me. You're a vital man. You could still have a family with someone."

Daniel listened. It seemed as though Gretchen was sputtering, but she was choosing her words wisely. She'd obviously been giving the subject a lot of thought. He waited until there was a minute of silence between them. He placed his glass down and brought his hands on either side of her arms.

"You haven't said it, and I'm fine with that, but you heard me the other day. In case you don't remember because you think you're so old, I said I loved you. There's no condition on that statement. I just love you. I want you. You and all your nonsense, and sometimes it is only that, is who you are, and I love every part of your mind, and especially that luscious body. You're always surprising me. You've brought me out of darkness, and I can't thank you enough for that."

Gretchen smiled slightly. "But, you love children. You help all of those kids at the center."

"Yes, but I'm with you, and my eyes were wide open when you and I got together. I figured we wouldn't have a family. Gretchen, you are my family. Now, let's have a good time tonight."

Gretchen only nodded. "They have a signed football over there if you're interested."

"What's the bid at? Is it signed by all of them? How about Coach?"

"You are such a child. Yes, all of them including the coach. I think the bid was two hundred dollars."

"I bet I can get that baby for five hundred." He walked away talking numbers. Gretchen followed. *What a man I have!*

Luckily, Gretchen and Daniel were seated with her good friends the mayor and his wife, and two other couples Gretchen knew from other events over the years. Daniel directed his attention to the booklet at each place setting that explained the charity, the programs, and the live auction items for the evening.

"Well, Detective, did you see something?" Miranda Jacquard asked. "These auctions can go into the millions."

"I saw a couple of trips, and then there's this sports car."

"What kind of salary do you have on the police force?"

Daniel stiffened against the mayor's wife's question. "I save. I'm a saver."

"Oh, okay," Miranda said with a smile. "I can appreciate that. You have to be able to spend some money or you couldn't keep up with our dear Gretchen."

Gretchen stepped in. "Daniel is very generous to a fault, but we love to eat at home. I'm really a homebody with very simple tastes."

The entire table erupted in laughter. Gretchen feigned surprise. "What? I am. I only care about a good pair of stilettos."

Thankfully for Daniel, the dinner and program began. Gretchen spied Mrs. Notte's attorney. They nodded their hellos as the auction began. Gretchen looked over the items Daniel had marked.

"You can't afford that," she whispered into his ear. "Remember, Detective?"

"If I can get it for a good price, I can."

"Daniel, don't blow your cover. If they all discover you have money, your life will never be the same. Trust me on this. I know my people."

It was one thing to bid on items silently. It was another thing to have the entire room see a mere detective bidding on a luxury trip to St. Croix. Besides, he had his own island. But, it wasn't until he saw Gretchen's interest piqued, that he planned to raise his paddle. The bidding for a ruby bangle bracelet began at ten thousand dollars. No one in the room bit. It was lowered to eight thousand, but still there was no interest.

Miranda leaned over to the elite planner. "I saw that bracelet in New York last fall. It is stunning."

Gretchen looked as though she needed to wipe drool from her chin. "It is magnificent."

"What is wrong with these people?" Daniel asked out loud. He cleared his throat and yelled out. "Seven thousand dollars."

Gretchen hit him hard on the arm. "What are you doing? I have bracelets."

"The man at table two bid seven thousand, do I hear eight?"

Daniel lowered his head to murmur into her ear. "You don't have this one. I'm buying you a bracelet. I know the designer. It's a good deal at seven thousand."

"No, don't."

"Eight thousand, I have eight. Sir, will you do nine thousand?"

Daniel nodded.

Gretchen put her head in her hands. "Daniel, you are outing yourself."

"I don't care. It's for you. I'll do the original ten thousand for the charity."

"Oh no," Gretchen muttered. She looked over at Hal's wide eyes. When the auctioneer yelled "sold" and told Daniel the bracelet would be in the VIP area, she simply smiled.

"Detective, do you have a side hustle?" Hal asked as the table guests remained in shock.

"Actually, I do. You see Ms. Malloy is dating the heir to a diamond company, me."

"And you're a detective on our police force?" Hal was incredulous. "Why?"

"Because he's a good man," Gretchen answered quickly. "He wants to give back to the community, and I've never met anyone quite like him." She grabbed Daniel's face with both hands and kissed him soundly. After she finished, she intimately wiped the lipstick from his lips with her fingers.

"Wow, did not see that coming," Hal joked. "I didn't see the heir thing or the fact that you make one of my dearest friends very happy. Good for you, Detective."

"And, Mr. Mayor, Daniel almost solely supports that community center. You need to step it up."

"Yes, Gretchen. Detective, I'm sure you know by now, you just tell her yes. It's easier that way. You and I will talk about what we need to do for the kids. Let's have lunch next week."

"That will be fine, Mayor."

Gretchen draped a possessive arm around his shoulders. "And so it begins," she whispered into his ear. "Everyone will want a piece of Detective Williams now. This will be around the entire room before we leave tonight, and you'll probably pick up several phone numbers from some lovely younger women."

"And?" Daniel's eyes met hers.

"And I'll be crushed if you leave me, but I'll understand. Remember those children you could have?"

Daniel turned his face, his forehead touching hers. "And I'll be crushed if I leave you. Shut up and enjoy the bracelet. If I need a child that bad, we'll adopt."

"Daniel, I'm not sure about that."

"Me either so let's just enjoy the life we have."

The suggestion almost brought Gretchen to tears. There was a brief break in the auction. "Daniel, I saw Mrs. Notte's attorney. He and his wife are in the VIP area. I thought I saw something."

"Let's go. What did you see?"

"I'm not sure, but I have this hunch."

Gretchen's hand flew to her mouth as she gasped. She pointed at who she assumed was the attorney's wife.

Daniel shook his head. "Don't tell me that's the real necklace around her neck."

"You're the jewel expert. Is it real or a knockoff?"

"Honey, I need to get closer. Let's talk to them."

Gretchen took his hand and walked like a projectile meeting a target.

"Mr. Gilliard, how are you? Is this your lovely wife? Isn't this a wonderful event?"

"Ms. Malloy, this is my wife Marilyn, and yes, it's a great night. I guess you have a new bracelet coming your way." He nodded toward Gretchen's companion.

Daniel held Gretchen back and stepped forward to extend his hand. "I'm Gretchen's boy toy, Dee Williams. I'm in town from New York City. She said you're an attorney."

"Yes, we just met. I'm the lawyer for a friend of hers."

Gretchen nodded. "Honey, I told you about Mrs. Notte."

Daniel smiled at Marilyn Gilliard. "You ladies are lovely this evening. I love a beautiful piece of jewelry, and I truly admire that necklace."

The woman was pleased with her admirer. "Thank you. It was a gift from my husband. It is amazing."

Daniel stepped closer. "May I? I'm always interested in something beautiful. It only enhances your own beauty, Mrs. Gilliard."

"Please call me Marilyn. Since you can appreciate a fine piece of jewelry—"

And with that the woman removed the necklace and placed it in Daniel's hands. "This is exquisite, Marilyn. Every single stone is just perfect. Darling, you need to see this. There're even a few mine cut diamonds. See?"

Gretchen knew jewelry but didn't have Daniel's keen experience. "Lovely. Where on earth did you purchase this? I've seen a few items like this at very exclusive estate sales."

"It was actually an insurance private sale," the lawyer said proudly. "They haggled a little, but I won in the end."

Daniel looked up. "This is a real artisan piece. You were very lucky."

"Hey, Dee, can you get us deals on jewels? I'd like to get Marilyn earrings to match that piece."

"Oh, you'd be hard pressed to do that, but I could probably get you some diamond drop earrings at wholesale price. I'll be in Boston next week, and I have a guy. Funny, I deal with insurance companies too."

"It's the best way," Gilliard admitted as he held his now full glass of wine in the air. "It's a little shady, but a deal is a deal, right?"

Gretchen only smiled. She noticed Daniel was silent as well. He handed the piece back to Marilyn. "Thank you. That was a real treat to see something like that. Gretchen, would you like a refill on your champagne?"

"Of course, darling. But first will you take a photo of the Gilliards with me?"

"That would be lovely." The attorney's wife was giddy to stand next to Gretchen Malloy. "I've admired you so much Ms. Malloy."

Gretchen quickly took her place next to the woman. Her husband was requested rather adamantly to stand at his wife's other side. He looked less pleased, but Daniel took the photo quickly on his phone.

"Mr. Gilliard, let's get the ladies a refill."

Gretchen continued light conversation with the attorney's wife as the two men walked near the bar.

"This is a good photo, don't you think?" Daniel showed his phone to the man next to him.

"Yes, nice."

"And don't you think this is a lovely piece too?"

With the next photo, the attorney looked up at Ms. Malloy's companion. "What's this about? That's my wife's necklace."

"No, that's an imitation. The necklace on your wife's neck is one of Mrs. Notte's, but I think you already know that."

"It doesn't matter. Mrs. Notte doesn't care."

"It does matter, sir." Daniel opened his jacket and removed his badge. "I'm Detective Williams and you and I will be meeting tomorrow morning. I'll be at your office at ten sharp. If you aren't there, I'll put out an APB for you. Is that understood?"

"I bought it fair and square."

"From whom?"

"That insurance guy. It was all above board."

Daniel shook his head. "You know damn well it wasn't. Get your drinks and enjoy what little of the night you have remaining. I should have you picked up right now and taken down for questioning, but I'm going to trust that as an agent of the court, you **will** be there tomorrow morning. I'll expect the documentation, anything you have on this insurance man and on that necklace. By the way, how much did you pay for it?"

"Eight thousand."

Daniel snorted. "You didn't get a good deal, you stole it. Oh, and bring the necklace. It's evidence, but I won't embarrass you with your wife, not tonight. Remember, ten at your office tomorrow morning."

The attorney pulled out his phone and placed the time in his calendar. Daniel grabbed the cell. "And here's my number just in case you need a ride to your own office." As he handed it back to its owner, Gilliard's hands were shaking. *You should be very afraid. You could lose everything.*

Daniel turned and grabbed Gretchen's champagne. He grabbed a bottle of water for himself. "Have a great night, Mr. and Mrs. Gilliard."

The attorney glared. Daniel retrieved Gretchen. Marilyn was still beaming from all of the attention.

"I don't think she has a clue about the necklace." Gretchen took her glass happily. "Now what?"

"He and I will meet tomorrow morning. He knows something."

"It's that insurance guy isn't it? I have his name and phone number in one of my files. Gilliard's own assistant thought it was important and gave it to me as I was leaving the office."

"I'll take a look at it when we get home."

Gretchen clutched his arm. "You're coming home with me, Daniel?"

"Yes, if you'll have me."

Gretchen slid her tongue over her lips. "Have you? Dear man, you're already mine. In fact, we should go home right now."

"No more bidding? I saw a cruise. I've always wanted to visit Alaska."

Gretchen shook her head. "Nope. Too cold, Daniel."

"I can think of a few things to keep us warm. Don't you want to see moose, the Northern Lights, or salmon swimming in a stream?"

Gretchen headed back to the table to gather her wrap, purse, and to say her goodbyes to the table mates. "I can go to our very fine zoo to see moose, I prefer theater lights, and I can grill my own salmon."

Daniel stood his ground and stopped Gretchen's progress. "I have to pay for a bracelet, you say your goodbyes, and I'll meet you right here." He pointed down to the floor. "Here."

Gretchen mimicked him comically. "Here. Got it."

The auction began again as Daniel and Gretchen made their way out of the event. He'd called for the car while he paid for the bracelet, and it was waiting for them at the exit.

Daniel pulled the box from his pocket after they were settled in the backseat. "For you."

"Seriously? I just thought you did this as part of the act. Aren't you going to resell it?"

Daniel revealed the bracelet and pulled it out. "Give me your wrist."

Even though she rarely did as she was commanded, Gretchen held out her arm. Daniel placed the rubies on her arm and latched it shut. He kissed the inside of her wrist at the closure. "I like treating you."

"And I like you treating me too." She kissed him on the cheek and touched his cheek with hers. "I will treat you when we get home."

"I'm counting on it. I missed out on my Alaskan cruise."

Gretchen's laughter filled the car. "Oh honey, I'm way better than a boat with a few icebergs."

Daniel smiled. "The last ship that met an iceberg had a tragic ending, G."

As Gretchen examined her new jeweled accessory, she smiled. "Daniel, if I had been there I would've looked at that iceberg and made it melt."

"Is it suddenly hot in here?" Daniel asked as he fingered the buttons at his collar.

Gretchen slapped at his hands. "Here, let me do that. I didn't notice any temperature change," she purred purposefully. "This tie needs to come off too. Daniel, you seem tense."

As Gretchen kissed the side of his neck, Daniel tried to stay in control. "Maybe I'm just tired." *That's a good answer.*

Gretchen's finger outlined his lips. Her own lips were just inches away. "Then, we better get you to bed."

Daniel felt her breath as a warm subtle breeze. *Now that was a really good answer. Lord, help me.*

Chapter Nine

Leaving Gretchen in the morning was more difficult this Sunday than ever before. After last night, he had resolved that the woman was much better than an Alaskan cruise. He could see moose at the zoo, and he knew she could grill one fine piece of salmon. Gretchen remained asleep as he found a pair of jeans, button-down shirt, and a jacket he'd left in one small area of her closet. She'd offered him one drawer in the bathroom, one more in her bedroom, and three inches of space to hang a few items under her special shelving that housed her four-inch heels. *Who has a shelf devoted to just a certain height of heels? Gretchen. What did Dev call her, oh yeah, the stiletto terrorist.*

He kissed her on her forehead, but she reached up and kissed him softly on the lips. "Be a good detective. Come back soon. I'll be waiting right here."

"Right there, huh? I'm taking your car."

"You know where the keys are. My bracelet and I will still be right here."

Daniel chuckled. *For a woman who didn't want that piece of jewelry, he did receive a very nice thank you for it.*

He stopped at a drive-thru for a coffee and arrived at the attorney's office with a few minutes to spare. Assuming

Mr. Gilliard was already there, Daniel turned the knob to the office door and showed himself in.

"Mr. Gilliard? It's Detective Williams." The door into the interior of the large office was wide open. "Mr. Gilliard?"

Daniel had a very bad feeling. He removed his gun from its holster and tapped against the door. There was still no answer, but he noticed all of the lights were on. He looked behind the door and walked slowly near the desk. He saw shoes on the floor behind the leather office chair.

"Damn." The attorney's body was sprawled on the floor. William Gilliard was dead. The detective immediately made a call. His second call was to his partner. "Jerry, I need you to get over to a residence. I just found that attorney's dead body in his office, but his wife will be home. I'm texting you the address. She needs protection. Don't tell her anything, but it has to do with that girl we questioned the other day, Lolly. Put an APB out for her too. She better be at that apartment where we dropped her off."

Daniel crouched down to take a look at the body. From the man's eyes and the bruising around the neck, he knew the man probably was strangled, and it had occurred several hours ago.

"What the hell is going on?"

He heard a man's voice in the outer reception area. "Hello? Mr. Gilliard?"

Daniel's gun was seen by the man before he was. "Detective Williams?"

"Barrett? What are you doing here?"

"Mr. Gilliard told me to be here at ten this morning. He phoned me last night."

"Did he? Sit down. You and I are going to have a talk. You know something, and you're going to tell me."

Barrett dropped down onto the small sofa. He threw up his hands. "Why does everyone always assume the butler did it?"

"Because they show up in an office where the man they're supposed to meet is now dead." Before Daniel received an answer, a young woman walked into the office. Her eyes were trained on her cell phone.

When she finally looked up, she screamed out loud. "What is going on? No one is supposed to be here on a Sunday."

"Then what are you doing here?" Daniel secretly held his gun behind his back.

"I work here for Mr. Gilliard. I'm his assistant."

"Again, why are you here on a Sunday?" Daniel persisted.

"He called me last night and told me to get here around ten. I'm a little late."

"Ms–"

"Diana Bloome."

"Ms. Bloome, I'm Detective Williams and this is–"

"Mrs. Notte's man," she answered quickly. They both smiled at each other as if they were friends.

"Your boss has been killed. He's in his office. Please remain out here." Daniel finally showed his gun and returned it to his holster under his coat.

Tears came to the woman's eyes, and she almost fell into the nearest chair. "Oh my God. When? How?"

"We're not sure yet. Mr. Barrett, it is your last name, right?"

The man nodded. "Winslow Barrett."

Daniel continued. "He was asked to meet here too. Do you have any idea why he wanted you here?"

She shook her head quickly and cried out. "No! He just told me it was important. I thought it had to do with Mrs. Notte and that Ms. Malloy, her investigator."

Daniel tried not to roll his eyes, but they just automatically performed the action. "Ms. Malloy isn't an investigator, she's just a friend."

"Oh no, Detective. You saw her in her element at the mansion the other day," the butler countered. "Remember when she blew open that murder of one of her grooms, oh and she also was involved in that investigation of the bombing of the department store. I believe she's just begun her private investigating business, but she's been very successful."

Daniel turned away and took several deep breaths. *Why do I care about that insane woman?*

"Look, Ms. Bloome, did anything unusual happen on Thursday or Friday?" he began as he turned toward the young sobbing woman once again. "Maybe someone unusual came into the office besides Ms. Malloy?"

"She didn't come in then."

"Fine." *I'm absolutely getting nowhere.* Daniel heard the sirens pull up to the building. On a quiet Sunday morning, the noise filled the office like a full percussion delegation from the symphony.

He looked out and saw several patrol officers setting up a perimeter. He also noticed Jerry getting out of his car. "You two, don't move, and leave this door open." He pointed at the main office entry.

Daniel met Jerry in the hallway. "Do you have a car at Mrs. Notte's too?"

"Yes, they're there already. The car is at the lawyer's house too, and the coroner is right behind me. What the heck is going on?"

"I was supposed to meet the man at ten. He asked Mrs. Notte's butler to be here, and then he requested his assistant to come into work, but she was a little late. Gilliard looks like he's been strangled, but I have no idea how long ago."

Jerry nodded. "Oh, Lolly has been picked up, and she's headed downtown. You or I will question her as soon as we're finished here."

Daniel shook his head. "Everything changed last night. His wife was wearing the real necklace, the one that was fenced. We were going to talk about it."

"I'd die before I talked with you too." Jerry began to pass his coworker. "You can be a real hard ass."

"Apparently, I missed something, and it cost Mr. Gilliard his life."

"Nope, the man did something that cost his life. You had nothing to do with it. Now, let's go to work."

What has Gretchen stumbled onto this time? Maybe she is a super sleuth? I'll never tell her.

Chapter Ten

"Hello," Gretchen mumbled. She wiped her eyes as she answered the phone. Sleeping in on a Sunday morning was one of her favorite things to do. Now, if only Daniel hadn't left her alone…

"Gretchen, it's me. Help me."

Gretchen sat up in bed. "Mrs. Notte? What's wrong? You sound…are you hurt?"

"I'm hurt, and Barrett isn't here."

"I'll call 9-1-1. I'm on my way. Hang in there. Just stay on the line. No, I have to call. Hang up. I'll be there."

Before the woman could answer, Gretchen ended the call and hit the emergency number. "Yes, there's an elderly woman in dire straits at–"

She threw back the covers and headed to her closet. Throwing on her favorite yoga pants and hoodie, Gretchen slid on her sneakers and grabbed her bag. She continued to tell the operator what she knew and mostly what she didn't know.

As she headed to the parking lot, she saw her empty parking place. "Damn. Daniel has my car." Always prepared, Gretchen proceeded to the apartment lobby's concierge desk.

"Ms. Malloy, what can I do for you this morning?" Geraldine, one of the part-time employees, was ready to help.

"I need a ride. There's an emergency."

The young woman looked at her watch. "Ms. Malloy, I'm off the clock in—"

Gretchen's impatience could be heard in her tapping foot. "What? I'll just call a car."

Geraldine pointed at her watch. "Now." She pulled her purse from beneath the next. "Let's go. I'll drop you off."

"Oh, thank you. This is very important," Gretchen acknowledged. *Daniel and I must come up with a better solution for times like this. I cannot be blindsided again.*

By the time Gretchen reached the mansion, the ambulance was pulling into the driveway. She thanked Geraldine and exited the car quickly to inform them who she was. A police car pulled in behind. Gretchen tried the door, but it was locked.

"I can't get in. She's in there alone. Her assistant is away."

"What's happened?" the policeman asked as he checked the door again.

"I don't know, but I know she's in trouble. Things have been happening that have no explanation. She's...just help her."

Another officer tried a window, setting off the alarm. Eventually, the window lifted, and he crawled into the house. Once the front door was wide open, Gretchen gasped at the sight.

Mrs. Notte lay at the bottom of the staircase. There was a small pool of blood near her head. Immediately, the paramedics went to work. The elderly woman was just barely alive. In a matter of minutes, she was on the gurney to begin her trip to the hospital. She opened her eyes briefly and looked directly at Gretchen.

"Mrs. Notte, I'm here. You're going to be fine." Mrs. Notte tried to reach up. Instead, Gretchen leaned down. "You concentrate on getting well, and we will find out who is doing this."

As she was loaded into the ambulance, Gretchen stood helplessly behind. *What can I do?* She looked back at the blood at the base of the stairs. She began to photograph every area of the foyer and landing.

The police performed a light search around the house. "Aren't you going to do a more thorough investigation?" Gretchen stopped one of the officers at the front door.

"Why? The old lady fell down the stairs."

"She wouldn't be up there if her majordomo was away from the house."

The man shook his head. "What's a majordomo?"

"Never mind. Will you all be staying until he returns?"

"No. You're on your own. She's your friend."

Gretchen motioned toward the front door. "We can't just leave the house open."

"Then lock up behind you."

Gretchen stomped her foot. With sneakers instead of heels, her temper tantrum's muffled noise had no effect. "The alarm is turned off because you came in through the window and you told the security company you were on site."

"Lady, there's nothing more we can do. This was an accident, plain and simple. She shouldn't be living here on her own."

Gretchen squinted. Her anger was brewing, but she had to keep it together to help Mrs. Notte. "I'll stay here until her assistant returns. Thank you, officer, for all you've done." *And haven't done! I'll remember his name and tell Daniel at the appropriate time.*

The officers left, the cars vanished, and Gretchen was left alone in the house. As long as she was there, she might as well look around. Maybe she'd find something that might help. Her main focus was the office. There she found Mrs. Notte's chair knocked over and two crooked paintings on the wall.

"There was a struggle here." Gretchen photographed the entire room. She searched for a wall safe but found none.

Her next stop was the sitting room with the exit out to the garden. There was a cold breeze, and it was coming from a slightly ajar door. Either the officers forgot to close it, or someone had managed to enter through that area of the house again. Again, she took her photos. She looked around the kitchen and dining room. Her search took her to two more rooms on the first floor including a small library.

Gretchen walked up the staircase and took several photos of the landing. She examined every bedroom and sitting room on the second floor. Nothing seemed to be disturbed. She looked behind several photographs and wall art but didn't find a safe. If the burglar had wanted access to the safe, he would have to know the location and the combination.

Gretchen headed downstairs. She made sure every door was locked. The number for the security company was listed by the panel. She called them and waited for them to arrive. It was nearly one in the afternoon before they left the house, and Barrett finally walked into the house.

"Ms. Malloy? What is going on?"

She explained the "accident" and that Mrs. Notte had been transferred to the hospital on The Plaza. When the man saw the blood, he sat down on the stairs and began to sob. Gretchen only knew to sit beside him and place a comforting arm around the faithful employee. She was surprised to look up and see Daniel.

"Gretchen?"

"Daniel?"

"Honey, why are you here?"

"Mrs. Notte fell. She's in a bad state, Daniel. I'll tell you later. But why are you here?"

"I followed Barrett. The attorney is dead."

Gretchen was completely confused. "Mr. Gilliard is dead?"

"Murdered. Strangled. He called Barrett to come into the office at the same time he and I were supposed to have our meeting, and he asked his assistant to come in a little earlier, but she was late."

"Daniel, you know what this means, don't you?"

"Yes, there is more going on here than a confused elderly rich woman having an accident."

Gretchen stood and took Daniel by the hand. "There was a struggle in the office. The police didn't even care about it. I took their names, and I'll expect you to have a word, or several with them. They decided it was an accident, that she fell down the stairs. See?"

Daniel looked around the office. "There's no way she'd have it look like this."

"And they said she fell down the stairs, but there's no way she would've been walking down those steps without Barrett with her. She told me that the other day. Whoever came in knew he wouldn't be here."

Daniel began to look behind the wall art. "He was pulled away on purpose. Have you found a safe?"

"No. I even looked upstairs."

Daniel thought about the obvious. "We could go in the other room and ask her assistant where it is."

"The man is distraught, besides, where's the fun in that, Daniel?"

"True. Let's try to find it on our own for a few minutes. If I were rich," Daniel murmured and winked in her direction, "I'd probably put the safe in here. What doesn't match with the room?"

A lightbulb went off over Gretchen's head. "Wait. The other day, her eyes kept averting to this wall. In my years of studying people, I know when they're distracted, and it's usually the place where they don't want you to go. Something is off. Yes, like that panel right there that doesn't line up with the wainscoting?"

"Exactly." Daniel ran his hand along the line of the wood until he felt something. The chair rail popped open revealing a small safe, one that was long and thin. "Now, to open this baby."

"Maybe Barrett has the combination?"

Daniel leaned his head down upon the lock and began to turn the knob. "Don't need it. It's an oldie. I can handle this."

"My, you are full of surprises, and I adore a bad boy."

Daniel offered a smoldering glance with his soft gray eyes. "Of course you do. Down girl." Less than a minute later, Gretchen's detective popped the safe open and began to look inside at several documents including original wills and trusts. He removed a stack of cash and a small box filled with jewelry. "So, what does whoever want?"

"I think they want Mrs. Notte out of this house permanently," Gretchen announced plainly. "The attorney thought she should sell the house and move into a smaller home. Now, she's had a life-threatening accident. The home could be an endangerment to her."

Daniel sat on the edge of the desk. "But why? I can see talking to her about moving if the attorney was concerned about her welfare, but he apparently was pushing?"

"Yes. Mrs. Notte said he was over at the house almost once a week since she changed that will."

Daniel rolled his tongue to the side of his cheek in thought. "Maybe it's something in the will? We seem to be back to that, and that damn necklace."

"Oh, Daniel, what about his wife? Is she okay?"

"There's a patrol watching the house, and Jerry sent over a female officer to talk to her." Daniel's phone rang. "Jerry? What's up? Okay. How much footage? Do we have our guy? Do we have someone at the hospital with Mrs. Notte? Good. I'm sending Mr. Barrett there to be with her and setting up a perimeter here too. I just have this feeling. I'll catch up with you."

Gretchen fell into the chair in front of her detective. "It's exhausting being in your world, but I'm so glad you're in it. You're a very good cop."

"Thanks, darling. Now, let's get Barrett to the hospital to be with his lady. You need to go home." Daniel shook a finger in her face.

Gretchen began to say that one should never place a finger in her face if one still wishes to use said finger, but she clamped her mouth tightly. She nodded. "I will go home. Keys please." Her new bracelet hung off of her extended arm. "Besides, this just doesn't go with my outfit, does it?"

Daniel reached in his pocket and filled her open hand. "I don't know. It seems to go with everything you wear, and especially when you wear nothing at all. Come on. You can drop me off at my car first," Daniel directed.

"Of course, Detective Williams," Gretchen purred. *He said to go home, but he didn't say I couldn't continue my investigation. Besides, I need an associate on my team, and I know just the woman for the job!*

Chapter Eleven

"No. I'm not coming."

Gretchen leaned her head back on the couch and mimicked her friend. "No, I'm not coming. When did you become such a grump?"

Lily Schmidt Pierce, hit the bed with her hand. She couldn't scream or she'd wake the baby in her arms. Emi had just fallen off to sleep, and Andrew the terrible toddler was down for his afternoon nap. "I'm thinking it happened just the other day. I was going on two hours of sleep because Andrew had a bad cold, and the baby was waking me every two hours to feed. Not to mention, Dev had a quick trip down to Miami for some operation with the DEA. Yes, that's when I became a grump."

"But Mrs. Notte needs you." Gretchen thought if she could play the sympathetic, empathetic card, Lily would break.

"No."

"Lily, this is the perfect time. Perhaps Dev's father could take care of our little Drew for a few days, and the baby is perfect for bringing along. Emi is totable, portable, and you're her human vending machine. Easy."

Lily clenched her fist and pounded into the mattress. "It is not easy. She's less than two months old. I'm supposed to fly with an infant, leave my son here, comfort Mrs. Notte, and help you with what exactly?"

"The investigation. My heavens, have you lost your brain?"

Just the other day, Dev said the exact same thing. While she was pregnant, she did have a glitch in her thought processes. Had it continued after birth? "What could I possibly do?"

"It would be like the old days, you and me together."

"Get Abby," Lily answered quickly. Her former stalwart assistant remained in Kansas City and ran the flower shop.

"Abby has never been on a stakeout with me before. You have."

"I was watching a house, and you barged in as I recall."

Gretchen flipped her hair. "That's not how I remember our amazing adventure."

Through the monitor, Lily could hear and see Andrew stir. "Gretchen, I have to go. Keep me informed about Mrs. Notte. I'm sorry. I just can't." Before Gretchen could continue the conversation Lily hung up quickly. *I dodged a bullet with that one.*

"What is wrong with my old bestie?" Gretchen asked out loud. "How can she just ignore the dire straits that poor old Mrs. Notte is in? How can she just ignore my pleas?"

Back in Virginia, before Lily could reach her son's room, Dev was there picking Andrew up and headed to their bedroom.

"You're not going to believe what Gretchen wanted me to do?"

"I can only imagine, and it still won't even be in the ballpark." Devlin Pierce cradled his son. Andrew wasn't awake completely, but certainly wanted to snuggle against his father. In the last few weeks, the little guy had felt like he'd been displaced in his mother's eyes, replaced by a small body that did nothing but cry, eat, sleep, and poop.

"She wants me to come to Kansas City. Mrs. Notte has taken a bad spill down the stairs and is in the hospital. Her own attorney has been murdered, and before that he was insisting she sell her home and move to a home that would be safer for her. Then, there were some weird things like the bullet hole I told you about, an intruder in the house, and a necklace that was stolen and replaced with a fake. Apparently, the attorney's wife was wearing the real one last night. Daniel was supposed to have a meeting with him this morning, and he discovered him dead. It was probably strangulation. Oh, and Gretchen has a new ruby bracelet."

Dev sat down on the bed, placing a now sleeping Andrew onto a pillow. He mulled all the information over. For now, he'd keep it to himself that Daniel Williams had already contacted him twice about his own suspicions. "How did she get a bracelet out of all of that?"

"Daniel bought it. It was an auction item, for a charity. Oh, and they had a fight, but they're good now."

"Lord, I leave for a few minutes and miss everything. So, why not go? I'm sure you would make Mrs. Notte feel better."

Lily blinked her very weary eyes. "Have you lost your mind?"

"No. Go. I know you have to take Emi with you, but Andrew could stay here with Dad and me. I have friends, remember? I bet the priest would even take a shift. Of course, Andrew would miss you, but maybe the break would be good for you and for him."

"My baby brain is getting worse, isn't it?"

Dev stroked his wife's back. She still wore her robe and hadn't showered since Friday. "Will you get mad if I say yes?"

"No," Lily lamented. "I know. One child is tiring; two children are exhausting."

"Set it up and go."

Lily shook her head. "No. It's too soon for Emi to fly. I know people do it, but I don't feel comfortable traveling. Her little immune system is growing. I will go, but not just now."

Dev understood. "But, what if something happens to Mrs. Notte, and you haven't seen her? Will you be okay with that?"

"I have to be. Besides, if that does happen, Gretchen may never speak to me again."

"There's always a silver lining." Dev's chuckle brought forth the pain from a solid left fist shoved into his upper arm. "Well? Wouldn't it be?"

"There are those days. I'm not sure how the woman who used to torment Abby and me when we worked with her on events wormed her way into our lives. But we're stuck with her now, for better or worse."

Dev leaned over and kissed his wife. "That phrase seems to guide several of us, doesn't it?" He opened his arms. "Give me the baby. You, go enjoy a shower. I've got this."

Lily freely handed over the sleeping baby. She gave her husband a peck on the cheek. "I love you so much."

"I love you, too, beautiful."

As Lily entered the bathroom, the first thing she saw was her reflection in the mirror. "Beautiful? If I have baby brain, that man has lost his mind completely." *Maybe I do need a break?*

Chapter Twelve

Three days later, Detective Daniel Williams sat at his desk. He had been looking at his computer screen for over an hour. He was missing something that would bring the entire case to completion, but what that something was couldn't be defined. He was frustrated. Jerry arrived at his desk.

"We've got him. They're bringing him."

Daniel threw his pen on the desk. "Thank God. Maybe we can get somewhere now."

"That footage from the law office shows him going in and coming out with the correct time stamp to go along with the time of death. His real name is Nathan Portage, and he's rumored to be a fence from Miami, Florida."

"So that's how the attorney's wife ended up with Mrs. Notte's genuine necklace?"

"Yep, and that woman wasn't happy with me when I picked that piece of jewelry up from her. She was pissed."

"We need to keep that secure. It's worth at least a quarter of a million dollars." Daniel pulled up the fence's photo. "Miami? I wonder–"

"What? What are you thinking?"

"I'm thinking I need to make a call." Daniel was

already hitting his phone's contact list. He waited through two rings.

"Agent Pierce."

"Devlin? It's Daniel in Kansas City."

"You mean this is Gretchen's detective?" Dev laughed as he made the joke.

"That too. "I'm sending you a mugshot of a fence we have in custody. We think he was involved in a murder of an attorney."

"Mrs. Notte's attorney?"

Daniel wondered if Gretchen had ever considered becoming a social meeting star. She definitely could spread news far and wide. "The same one. He was posing as an insurance agent. Do you have the photo?"

"Yes. This guy looks very familiar."

Daniel continued to read the screen. The man had worked for years in Miami. "Did you ever work in Florida? Look at the years he was in Miami."

"I remember. I know him. He was known as Buddy Portage then."

Jerry pointed at the two officers bringing in the suspect. "He's coming in right now. Any ideas? This thing has me completely stumped."

Dev cleared his throat. "Well, what does Gretchen think? Did I just say that out loud?"

Chuckling, Daniel answered yes. "Gretchen thinks that there's several working parts, but she has a suspect, well two of them."

"Don't say Garrett and Bernard Notte." Dev stared outside his office window. It was beginning to snow. Traffic in the nation's capital was always horrendous but add even an inch of snow and it would come to a standstill. *Can this day get any worse?*

"I won't say it, but she has a point. Here's what I have. The attorney was encouraging Mrs. Notte to leave that house. He wanted her out of there. I've checked his financials, and his accountant revealed he was amassing a great deal of money to purchase a house, a very large one. Then we have a great niece who runs away from home, and Mrs. Notte takes her in. Lolly steals the necklace, works with Mr. Miami to have a fake one made. She gets a percentage of what it's worth. She returns the necklace and gets back in Mrs. Notte's good graces. In the meantime, the fence is paid by the attorney. Now, he has the real one. There's a bullet hole in the window, marks on the floor where there shouldn't be any, incorrect prescriptions, and threats. Then the attorney's wife wears the real necklace, and Gretchen notices it."

"Of course she does. Gretchen can always pick out a good piece of jewelry."

Daniel nodded. "Yes, she can. I confronted the attorney. He agrees to meet me at his office at ten in the morning on a Sunday. When I got there, he was dead from strangulation. But he asked Mrs. Notte's butler to be there at the same time, and his assistant was to come a little earlier, but she was late."

"That's lucky for her. Is she involved?"

"I checked her out, but she's been cleared. Besides, when Gretchen began this investigation, Mrs. Notte had her meet the attorney to obtain copies of the old and the new will–"

Dev stood up. "Wait. She changed her will?"

"Yes, she changed it last year. It was after your trip last October to Anna Maria Island, Florida. As soon as she did that, little things began to happen. You need to know the assistant gave Gretchen the insurance man's name and number during that meeting, and she added other copies of trusts, etc. The day of the murder she freely gave us security tapes. That led to your Miami friend."

"Daniel, what's in that will? Do you know?"

"Yes, and so does Gretchen."

"How much of a change did Mrs. Notte make? Did she knock anyone off?"

Daniel wondered if he should tell Gretchen's secret. Actually, he remained surprised that she hadn't let the cat out of the bag to Lily. "You have to keep this between us. Gretchen can't know I told you. I'll send you both copies, but for now, her son and grandson are completely disowned. The majority of the property and money all goes to Angelica."

"I'll alert Carlos just in case," Dev said out of concern. "Is that it? Any surprises?"

"A few charities received donations, and that lovely beach house you all stayed at?"

"Yes, it's worth millions," Dev acknowledged. The home sat directly on the beach, facing out on the Gulf of Mexico with a pool and hot tub. Three stories high, the house accommodated twelve comfortably, but could hold double that number.

"Well, Barrett the butler is to retire there and manage the property for as long as he lives or wishes, and the woman who inherits it is...your wife."

The snow was falling faster, and Dev's day was not just worse, it was bad. "Lily? My Lily?"

"Yes, yours."

"But we can't, I mean how will that look? In my area of government work, you just don't inherit a house like that without your superiors going over your entire record."

Daniel could hear the stress in Dev's voice. "Wait. Hold on. You just have to show your bosses the will when that day comes. They'll put the information in your file. They'll do a little investigating, and you'll just go on like before."

"Only we'll own a very expensive beach house. You sound like a man who had to undergo the same procedure."

"My case was a little different. They couldn't understand why a rich guy wanted to work in Kansas City as a detective. It'll be fine, Dev."

"Except for the taxes every year, the maintenance, and the utilities—"

"Apparently, Mrs. Notte has set up an operating fund that will pay all of that for at least twenty years. You could always sell it after Barrett leaves or dies and imagine the rental income for a place like that with a manager on-site."

Dev hit his head with his hand. "I'm getting a headache, but that income could easily put the kids through college. Why Lily?"

"Hell if I know. You can't tell her though."

Dev knew, and he appreciated the advance information from Daniel. "I can keep a secret. Daniel, let me look at this guy and the dates he was working in Miami. I'll correlate it with our DEA files and see what I find. Send those wills and any of the other documents that are different from the first one. All of this has to be related, and quite possibly back to the father-son drug duo."

"That does seem to be the case. God help us."

Dev decided to broach one more subject. "Daniel, Gretchen wants Lily to come. She says it would do Mrs. Notte good. I think your lady wants to reunite the dynamic duo of florist and event planner private investigators."

"Dev, I think the truth is Gretchen misses your wife very much. Lily may even be like a little sister to her after all of these years. Do you know that the stiletto terrorist said she'd break it off with me because I'd probably want kids?"

Gretchen had a compassionate thought? Who knew she could do that? "Well, that was very thoughtful. What did you say?"

"I said we could adopt. She quickly nixed that."

Dev couldn't control his laughter. "Oh yeah. Auntie G is good for a few hours with her little Drew, but after that someone better be taking the little man off of her hands or she'll find a buyer for him."

"Lord, what have I gotten myself into with her?"

"Detective, I wonder about that almost every day. But, Daniel, seriously, I've never seen her more normal, if that's possible for Gretchen Malloy. Are you happy?"

"Strangely, yes. I love her. I've told her, but something seems to be holding her back. I try to understand because I prefer being with her, more than I can stand to be without her."

"I'll pray for you, Daniel. All I can tell you is to do what makes you happy and be with the one you love. It makes everything better. With what we do, we need someone there at the end of the day."

Jerry motioned for Daniel to head to the interrogation room. "I've got to go, Pierce. I'll send those copies to you before the end of the day. Thanks, and we will talk soon."

"Yes, we will." Dev sat back down and scrolled his computer screen. He saw a date that meant something to him. "I was in Miami then. I have to know this man but from what operation?"

He swiveled to watch the snow. *If he's not the one moving all of the chess pieces, I'd say it was who was inheriting, but that's a little girl...and my own wife!*

Chapter Thirteen

Valentine's Day came and went. Barrett continued to visit Mrs. Notte who was now in a rehabilitation facility, and he lived at the mansion. He'd hired a security team to watch for any movement twenty-four hours a day, seven days a week. Over the last four weeks, there wasn't one break-in or unusual occurrence. Upon the death of the attorney, all of the shenanigans came to a halt.

Gretchen's year of events and weddings were being planned with one small wedding and an anniversary party already in the book. Daniel was busy being a detective. But their relationship was still taking shape.

Life could become monotonous, but today was going to be spectacular, at least for Gretchen. Lily was coming.

"Daniel, you **will** be home by five, won't you?"

"Yes, Gretchen."

"Now, she and the baby will be tired, so you'll say hello, then you may change your clothes, and I'll have dinner ordered. You will leave and pick it up."

Luckily, Gretchen couldn't see him mimicking her while he listened. "Is this an itinerary that you've planned? It sounds like it."

"I appreciate a good schedule just like all good planners do. I just want everything to be perfect for her and the baby."

"Are they staying at the apartment?" Daniel continued his drive to the courthouse downtown. He was testifying in a murder trial of the suspect in the death of a young father who had been shot at a gas station.

"Of course. I want as much time with them as possible."

Daniel chuckled. "Darling, have you ever been around a baby full time?"

"Don't be ridiculous. I was around–" Gretchen stopped herself. *No, I only stayed an hour, but what about...no, I visited for a few minutes.* "It won't be a problem, Daniel. You worry too much."

"I suppose," Daniel answered, but he knew the truth. He knew Gretchen well enough by now to know when he'd guessed correctly. "I have to go, but I'll be there at five. I can't wait to meet both of them."

"You're just going to love Lily, well she is very different from me, but you'll overlook her rather regular looks and views on society, won't you?"

"We'll be fine. I like her husband so I'm sure I'll like her, and I can get along with just about anyone." *Even you, stiletto terrorist. I've learned to love you.*

Gretchen looked at the kitchen clock. "Oh my! They're landing. She's renting a car. I hope she can remember how to get here. Daniel, I can't be wasting my time talking. I need to make sure everything is ready. Goodbye."

"Good—" *She's hung up. She's already checked everything three or four times. I've never seen her this nervous, or have I ever seen her this way?*

Gretchen spent the next two hours pacing and searching the apartment for anything that might be out of place or unsafe for the baby. Eventually, she realized that the baby wasn't walking, maybe not even crawling yet. Lily texted they were on their way, but first she had to stop and grab a few items.

"You are always making me wait, Lily."

When the buzzer went off to announce her visitors' arrival, she nearly jumped out of her heels. Instead, she smoothed her dress and checked her face in the mirror. She opened the door as though she was an old movie actress allowing access into her mansion.

"Welcome to my home."

She looked out into the hallway to see the doorman lugging two bags and two more grocery sacks. Lily carried a child carrier, a purse, and another carryon. She puffed away a stray hair from her face, looking up and down at Gretchen's attire.

"Was I supposed to dress up? As early as we left this morning, this is all I could manage."

Gretchen examined. She hoped the baby was in the carrier. Lily wore a long, bulky sweater over jeans with her sneakers. There wasn't one patch of skin that had makeup on it. *That girl has never had a fashion sense. How did she acquire Mr. Delicious?* Gretchen smiled and gave her friend a kiss and hug. "You look absolutely wonderful. Randy, just bring the bags in here."

The man pushed past the reunion and headed to the kitchen area. "There's ice cream in this bag."

Gretchen waved with her hand. "You know what a freezer looks like. Just go ahead." She turned her attention to the blanket covered object. "You do have her in there, don't you?"

Lily grinned. "Of course. She and I are inseparable." She looked around at the picture-perfect home. She hadn't been here in what seemed like a lifetime. Placing the carrier on the floor near the couch, she dropped her carryon and crouched down to unveil her daughter. Emi's wide eyes were as sweet as her smile. As Lily lifted her up, the baby giggled. "And here she is."

Gretchen gulped. She felt the tears bubbling up in her eyes. "Oh my. She is absolutely beautiful."

"I've already changed her. She's as clean as she'll be. Do you want to–"

"Of course, I do." Gretchen's arms were already welcoming.

"Emi, this is your Auntie G."

Gretchen took possession of the infant. Emi looked at her and frowned. "I don't think she likes me."

"Give it time. It's been a long day."

Lily looked over to see a struggling doorman. "Let me do that. Thanks so much for helping us. It seems like it doesn't take a village to get me anywhere; it takes a tactical unit." She caught Gretchen and mouthed if she should give him a tip. No was the answer. Gretchen whispered she would take care of him.

While Lily stayed busy with her groceries, Randy left, and Gretchen sat down to acquaint herself with the Pierces' newest addition. "How is my little Drew?"

Lily grimaced. "**Andrew** is fine, but I'm not doing very well. I bawled like a baby this morning. He was still sleeping in the car when I walked into the airport. It was easier leaving Dev. That sounded very wrong."

"No, I understand. It's always a good thing to have a break. Men can be so, so overwhelming and frankly dense."

Lily placed the last item into the refrigerator. "Are we speaking of men in general or one detective in particular? Or, and please don't tell me, a former love and retired Marine?"

"I haven't heard from Chance since Christmas. He sent a very nice card." Gretchen looked down at Emi's toenails. "We should paint your daughter's nails."

"No."

"But I have the perfect shade of red–"

"Of course you do, but no." Lily nearly fell onto the couch. "Now, what's the poor detective done now?"

Gretchen huffed. "Sincerely, why must you think he's done anything?"

Lily wiped her dry eyes. "Then, you've done something stupid?"

"Lily! How can you possibly say such a thing? I never do anything stupidly. I do things for impact."

Lily slipped off her sneakers. Gretchen was busy admiring Emi's long fingers. The baby was smiling at the woman with the long hair. "And for attention. I should have asked if you've exhibited some outrageous behavior that the man didn't appreciate?"

"Lily, really. I'm not outrageous." Gretchen winked at her friend. "Daniel will be here at five, and I've ordered your favorite barbecue."

"That sounds wonderful. The baby and I will need a quiet night to get us back on schedule. Dev and Andrew will call later before bedtime."

"How is Mr. Delicious?"

Lily's softened face gave her friend the answer. "He's still delicious. There're times when he's dense, but we get over that and go on. He's still not very fond of me researching or investigating local murders, especially when I find the mystery buried in our yard."

Gretchen handed Emi off to her mother. "Well, I have a fantastic mystery for you, and since we need to do everything we can for dear Mrs. Notte, I can't wait for you to see what I've compiled."

Emi snuggled in her mother's arms. Her eyes were heavy, and she soon closed them. Lily watched as Gretchen proudly presented a file folder in front of her.

"After acquiring a few pieces of information from Judge Stanwell...you remember him, don't you?"

Lily thought for a second. The name was familiar. Gretchen sat down next to her on the couch and sighed in frustration.

"You designed the flowers for his two daughters' weddings. The one girl was married next to that pond, and the bullfrogs were louder than the harpist."

Lily giggled. "Now, I remember. That was so funny, and you were out there trying to move the little suckers. You were coaxing them with those bacon canapés." Now, Lily's giggle turned into a full laugh.

"I was thinking about frog legs, and it wasn't that funny," Gretchen reprimanded. "You do remember now!"

"I liked them. They were nice, unlike their very demanding wedding planner."

Gretchen opened the folder. "That was me. You're not funny. Now, I put out a few feelers, and the judge came up with some very vital information. Apparently, Mrs. Notte's attorney had a nice little side job for additional income and to make his wife a very happy woman. Here's three complaints that came across for review."

Lily looked over her baby's head and read one of the papers. "So, the families were complaining that there was jewelry missing upon the death of their loved ones?"

Gretchen nodded as she looked over another sheet. "This one is a complaint about a missing antique French armoire that had been insured and appraised for over forty thousand dollars over ten years ago. The relative dies. The family arrives in town, and the piece of furniture is missing. Mr. Gilliard had collected the item and said that the client left it to him. On the other complaints, the jewelry was missing."

"That is funny. That's very coincidental and too many cases against one single attorney."

"It gets even funnier when you notice that probate went through the same judge. I think they were in league together. Now, add the fact that the same insurance company was used by **all** of the clients–"

"Wow. That's a conspiracy. I think you're really onto something." Emi shook in her mother's arms from Lily's exuberance. "Sorry, baby. Have you told your detective?"

Gretchen nervously made a clicking noise with her tongue. "Not yet, silly."

"Don't you think you should?"

Gretchen shut the folder. "Why must you do that?"

Lily smirked. "Do what?"

"Be you. I hate that."

Gretchen rose suddenly and took her folder with. Lily stayed where she was and remained confused. *I bet I could still get a hotel room just across the street.* The same hotel had served as the site of her wedding reception, short honeymoon, and the place Dev and she stayed whenever they returned to Kansas City.

"Gretchen, exactly what is wrong with me?" Lily thought she might as well ask while there was still time to pack up and get a room.

The other friend stood near her kitchen sink. "You're reasonable and honest. I'm not that way."

"Wow, that took a lot for you to admit that." Lily stood carefully trying not to wake her sleeping baby. She took her place across from Gretchen at the island. "Look, I've learned my lesson. I've been kidnapped, shot at, threatened, and I'm sure something will happen again in the near future considering all the digging into holes I shouldn't be in. I have Dev, Danny, JT, Paul, Ari, and even Dev's brother at times to keep me safe. His dad is always my rock, but Gretchen you have a man who obviously cares very much for you. You need to let him in, and please do not place yourself in jeopardy. You've done that enough already."

Gretchen heard Lily's words. *Lily has a point, but where is the fun in staying out of this?* "I didn't offer you anything to drink."

"It's fine. I'm fine. You know, I think I'll go get a room across the street. Dev and I love that hotel, and when the baby cries all night, I won't be worried that we've disturbed you."

Gretchen positioned herself with her two hands flat on the counter. "You will not. You'll stay here, and Emi and I can cry together. Now, what about wine?"

"First, I need to unpack and get her settled. I'll just put her in the carrier, and I brought this little nest thing that goes on the bed. Once I get that setup, I can relax, and I'll have a small glass of wine. Do you have white?"

Gretchen nodded, adding a smile. "I have your favorite. I can help."

By the time Daniel Williams opened the door to Gretchen's apartment, Lily had moved all of her luggage and baby gear to the guest bedroom at the other side of the apartment. Emi woke, was fed, and acquainted herself with Auntie G's hair. She would wound a long stand in her little fist and not let go. Lily had even had time to check in with her husband and have a short video visit with her toddler. His grandfather and his favorite priest were visiting so he had very little time for his mother.

As Daniel walked into the apartment, he was surprised to see a more casual Gretchen. And she held a baby. "Look what I have, Daniel. Isn't she a beauty?"

Indeed, you are. "I never ever expected to see a baby in this apartment. Hello ladies."

Lily stood and extended her hand. "I'm Lily Pierce."

"Lily, just give him a hug." Gretchen's joyful voice made way for Emi's giggle.

Lily pulled back her hand and began to move forward, but thankfully the detective went on the offensive to pull her into an embrace. "It is so good to finally meet you."

"Dev speaks fondly of you," Lily admitted. They both smiled genuinely at each other as they pulled apart.

"Ladies, I need to change since you all are pretty comfortable."

Gretchen shook her head at the baby girl. "I had to change. This one here spit up all over my outfit."

Daniel's brow raised. "And she lives?"

Lily chuckled. "Oh, you understand her very well."

Daniel laughed. "You have no idea how well. I'll change and pick up the barbecue. Excuse me."

He vanished as quickly as he arrived. Lily watched Gretchen as she played with Emi. "Does he live here now?"

"No, not always. He still has a tiny apartment, but he has space for a few of his garments." Gretchen's smile soured suddenly. "Lily, your daughter smells."

Emi was still delighted by her new friend and the lovely hair. Lily outstretched her arms, and the baby shook with the anticipation of being near her mother again. "Ari says she has the worst diapers ever." Lily's nose wiggled. "Yep, she smells. I'll change her and get her ready for bedtime. It may be a while. I might as well feed her too."

"Take your time. It'll be almost an hour before Daniel returns with dinner."

Daniel and Lily passed each other in the small hallway. Lily stopped him before he entered the living room. "Do you think she'll be okay with us here? I can go right across the street to the hotel."

Daniel leaned down to whisper. "She may not know what she's getting into, but she wants you and that baby here very much. Stay."

Lily nodded. "Detective, she has a theory about the lawyer. Make her tell you."

"I like you. You're a snitch."

Lily noticed that Daniel's gray eyes actually twinkled. "I only do it to Gretchen. The truth is, I think she's right."

"Thanks for the head's up. It's nice to have a man on the inside when it comes to Gretchen. Excuse me, a woman on the inside."

Lily began to walk to the guest room but stopped. "Detective, I'm so happy she has you in her life."

Daniel merely nodded and walked back into the lioness's den. He grabbed his car keys off the kitchen island and headed to the door. Before he did, he kissed Gretchen's cheek. "I'll be back as soon as I can."

Gretchen leaned her head back to look up to him. "I can't wait…for the barbecue."

Daniel ignored her joke and left quickly. Gretchen heard his laughter before he entered the elevator.

Chapter Fourteen

"Dear Lily."

Mrs. Notte's eyes filled with tears, but her smile was wider than her face as Lily entered the private room at the rehabilitation center. "Mrs. Notte, we've missed you." The two women embraced and held each other for a couple of minutes.

"And is that the baby?"

Gretchen held a smiling Emi but handed her quickly to her mother for Mrs. Notte's review. The elderly woman seemed to carefully examine the baby and nodded. "She has those same beautiful eyelashes like your husband."

"Yes, she does. There's no doubt that Emi and Andrew are his," Lily proclaimed proudly. "How are you doing? When will you be home?"

Mrs. Notte's smile vanished. "I'm not sure I'll ever leave this place. I don't seem to be improving."

Lily noticed the despondent tone in her voice. "It was a bad fall. It takes time even for someone half of your age. Just take it easy and improve every day."

Mrs. Notte placed her elbow carefully on the arm of the chair. She lowered her head and held it with her hand. "I just don't know."

Lily grabbed the woman's free hand. "I do. You need to get better. We should all meet again at the house on Anna Maria this summer. I'd love to see Alise and Carlos' baby, and don't you want to see your great granddaughter? Angelica loves you so much."

Mrs. Notte lifted her head and smiled. "You are very persuasive. I'm so happy to have her in my life and all of you. You should go to the house. It's yours to enjoy."

Lily patted her hand. "We did enjoy **your** house."

Mrs. Notte glanced at Gretchen. "Ms. Malloy, you haven't told her?" Gretchen nodded side to side. "You are very good at keeping secrets."

Lily threw a side glance at her friend. "Gretchen? What haven't you told me?"

"Mrs. Notte should be the one to do that."

Lily was completely confused. The usually talkative Gretchen was relatively quiet and completely content holding Emi. She also knew a secret and hadn't disclosed it. *That's not Gretchen. She must be sick.* "Mrs. Notte?"

"I've left you the beach house."

Lily gulped. "Excuse me?"

"I've left you the house upon my death. But I've been thinking. I want to transfer the ownership to you while you're here. I've already set it up so I want no discussion from you. The attorney, Ms. Malloy's gentleman, will be here in a few minutes. You'll have the deed within sixty days."

"No, no, no. I can't. Why would you do that? Leave it to Angelica."

"Dear girl, I'm leaving her so much. Your family and friends gave me such lovely memories last year. We had so much fun. You deserve it, Lily."

Lily's confusion grew. "A hitwoman was shooting at us."

Mrs. Notte's face seemed to light up. "Oh, it was exciting, wasn't it? Ms. Malloy, you should've been there."

Gretchen bounced Emi on her lap. "I do love a good crime mystery."

Lily turned and glared. "You aren't helping, Gretchen."

Gretchen stuck her tongue out at Lily. "I don't mean to. Take the house, Lily."

Mrs. Notte reached out for both of Lily's hands. "Dear Lily, you and your friends gave me an experience I'll never forget, and you have saved me from my son and grandson. Take the house. There is one stipulation. My dearest friend Barrett will retire there and be the on-site manager. He'll take the apartment below. You must agree he can stay as long as he wishes. Just think, you can rent it for an outrageous price. Two years ago, we rented it to a family from Germany for thousands. It's a fantastic investment."

"But we can't. Dev can't have a house that's worth millions." Lily's persuasive discussion was going nowhere.

"Dear Devlin won't have the house. You will. It will keep you secure for the rest of your life if you play it smart, and I have no doubt you will. When Barrett leaves or goes to meet his maker, sell it if you like. Then you'll be a millionaire. That's security."

Indeed, it is. Holy Moly! My life has just changed.

As if he was following a script, Barrett arrived as did Gretchen's own attorney and his assistant who was a notary. The papers were signed, notarized, and Lily assured all would be filed and the final deed would be on its way to her. Mrs. Notte was exhausted, and Lily and Gretchen knew it was time for them to leave.

For Lily, it seemed a kiss and hug wasn't sufficient as repayment to a woman who had floated into her life as a customer. All she had ever done for Mrs. Notte was to treat her nicely and befriend her in a very bad time. "Mrs. Notte, I'm not sure you realize what you have done for my family," Lily said as she hugged the woman and said her goodbyes.

"I know what I've done, and it is repayment for hours of love and delight. Thank you, Lily."

Once in the hallway, Barrett stopped the visitors. "Ms. Malloy, have you heard about my adventure?"

"No, but I love a good adventure," Gretchen answered coyly.

"The police are putting me up in a hotel for a couple of nights. They want the house empty. I believe they are doing one of those setup things."

"Sting," Lily and Gretchen answered in chorus.

"Yes, a sting. The house will be empty. They also had me tell everyone I could…the security people, Mrs. Notte's gardeners, our maintenance contractors, even club members. Maybe the bad guys will try to go after their treasure."

Gretchen winked at Lily. "Yes, maybe they will. Enjoy your hotel stay."

Once in Lily's rental car, Gretchen suggested they go for a late lunch on The Plaza at one of her friend's favorite restaurants. Gretchen had an idea, and now all she had to do was lure Lily into her plan.

Chapter Fifteen

"So Daniel is working late tonight?" Lily asked as she drove down Ward Parkway. This was one of her favorite streets and even in darkness it held a beauty unsurpassed by anything near her house in Virginia. She had always loved driving past the amazing, elegant homes. In the median along the parkway, there were ponds and fountains. When she was a teenager, her favorite area had been the Meyer Circle. It was an elaborate fountain and provided every driver who wanted to pretend to be in Monaco, the perfect opportunity to race around the roundabout.

"Yes. He usually heads to his apartment after his shift. He's very sweet to consider my sleep. You are driving a little fast."

"I love this circle. I've missed it. The best drive in Virginia is the George Washington Parkway, and it's a distance from us. I used to drive it to meet Dev for lunch once in a while before Andrew's birth."

"So, you're telling me you don't get out much? That's very depressing. I never thought you'd be happy with just a mundane little wifey life." Gretchen held on as Lily drove one final time around the circle.

"I don't have just a mundane little wifey life, Gretchen. I have responsibilities, unlike you who still lives the majority of her life off the cuff and in those blasted heels."

"Those heels have gotten me out of some tight places, and besides, they make my legs shapelier. Do you know Daniel once drank a shot of rum off of my calf as we–"

"La, la, la," Lily repeated over and over while Gretchen continued with her story. "I don't want to hear this. I'll never look at him with respect again."

"Oh, if you only knew!" Gretchen's laughter was low. She looked back to see Emi's eyes heavy with sleep. "You would respect him if you knew some of the things he can do."

"When will you stop that?" Lily continued to drive.

"Never. I'm not dead, unlike you. Surely, Mr. Delicious isn't boring."

Lily chuckled. "He certainly is not. I'm not going to discuss my love life with you."

"Fine, then let's just discuss your sex life, or I have a feeling it may be your lack of a sex life. Poor Devlin."

"Poor Devlin my–" Lily shut her mouth. Gretchen had goaded her just like the old days. "What are you up to?"

"Turn down that street with the statue on the median," Gretchen directed.

For some reason that Lily didn't really understand, she did as she was told. *It's just easier to go along with Gretchen.*

"Then turn right there and park the car. I have a suspicion that with the Notte family, the mango doesn't roll very far from the bush."

"It's an apple that doesn't fall far from the tree, not a mango," Lily reprimanded.

"Apple, mango…both are fruit."

Why are we friends? Lily turned away from Gretchen and also wondered why they were here facing the back of a garden, one that was surrounded by a black wrought iron fence. She turned off the car and looked behind her at a sleeping baby. "Emi always goes to sleep in the car. Andrew does the same thing. What are we doing here?"

Gretchen pointed at a very small gap in the fencing and the large hedge. "This is the back of Mrs. Notte's property. The police are probably staked out around the other block, but I figure that whoever is sliding into that house is coming through the garden. Mrs. Notte showed me smudges on the floor as though someone had entered from there. It was January. No one should've been in that garden, not even one gardener."

"I agree, but what are **we** doing here?"

Gretchen reached behind her and pulled a very large bag forward. "We are on a stakeout of our own, and this time I came prepared. The last time we did this, you didn't have any snacks or a thermos of coffee."

As Gretchen removed two covered coffee mugs and handed one to her, Lily knew her friend was at it again. "**We** did not **do** a stakeout. You tracked me down and scared me to death when you tapped on the blasted glass window with those fingernails. And you made enough noise with those heels to wake the dead."

"I don't remember it that way," Gretchen answered with a slight tone of indignation in her voice. "Well, I brought goodies. What do you want? I have candy bars, popcorn–"

"How long are we going to just sit here?"

Gretchen sighed, deeply and dramatically. "It won't hurt to sit for a bit, will it? We can visit."

Lily grimaced. "I suppose we can just sit here and talk. Emi is sleeping, and I'm just sitting. There are days when I don't sit down until it's almost time to go to bed. With a toddler and a baby, my days are filled with…what are you pulling out now?"

"Swedish goldfish. Do you want a few?"

"No. It looks like you packed for an army, Gretchen…maybe an army of clowns?" Lily took a sip from her coffee. Gretchen had remembered how she loved a caramel macchiato, and the beverage was still hot.

"If you're going to be on a stakeout, you have to eat like you're on one, or the stakeout is relatively a wash. You may quote me."

"Ha, kind of like you don't sweat, you glisten?"

"Exactly. I can be very quotable. Do you want cheese and grapes? I have small warm pizza rolls too."

Lily closed her eyes to pray. *Dear Lord, please tell me again why I'm friends with this outrageous woman? I remember. She volunteered to be kidnapped in my place because she said I wouldn't last in a harem. Why?*

When Lily opened her eyes, she held her hand out. "Hand over one of those pizza rolls."

"You've got it, bestie!" A delighted Gretchen proudly presented two individually wrapped in foil cheeseburger pizza rolls. "Isn't this fun?"

"Oh yeah, so much fun. Are you wearing stilettos?" Lily caught a reflection from a sequin on Gretchen's shoe.

"Yes, one should be fashionable while fighting evil."

"And how is one going to run in those things to capture the evil doers?" Lily asked smugly.

"I am not running. You are."

If these pizza rolls weren't so darn good! "Our big night out is to watch a fence and a large hedge to see if there's a little itty-bitty gap that someone could slip through. At least Emi isn't spitting up on me, so this is considered a good time."

"You need to get out more," Gretchen grumbled. "How's all the men in your life?"

"Well, Andrew and Dev are wonderful. Dev's dad is busy working on updating his kitchen cabinets. Dev's brother is living in Rome right now on loan to the Vatican."

"He's the art guy with the FBI, right?"

"Yes. Then the priest is the priest. He usually drops by every Sunday for dinner. Paul and his wife are solid. One girl is in college and the other is still in high school. Your favorite SEAL, JT comes and goes. He's back to Coronado this summer to be an instructor for something he can't talk about."

"What about that gorgeous Ari?"

"I have no idea. He sent gifts at Christmas, and a couple weeks after Emi arrived, a very large package came from London. Inside was the most beautiful christening gown, soft slippers, bonnet, and a light blanket. We looked up the store online, and the royals shop there. He spent a fortune on the outfit."

Gretchen licked her lips. "That man could spend a fortune on me anytime he wants."

Lily took a bite of the pizza roll. *Gosh, this is good.* "What about the detective?"

Gretchen waved her hand in the air dismissively. "Lily, you can never have enough handsome, wealthy men in your life. Ooh, you could quote me on that too. Sometimes, I can't help myself."

"That's for sure," Lily grumbled. "Now, let's talk about Daniel and Gretchen, K-I-S-S-I-N-G."

"Stop that immediately. We are not children."

"But sometimes it's fun to act like you are?" Lily winked in her "bestie's" direction. "You giggle when you're around him, and you flip that hair as if you're giving him a special code for—"

"Shhh. I hear something."

Lily chuckled. "That's rich. You just don't want to talk about a man who said he loves you. I believe you're afraid of commitment."

"Shhh. I hear footsteps, very familiar ones." Gretchen removed a small shovel from her bag.

Lily couldn't believe what she was seeing. *A shovel? When did she pack all of this stuff, and how did she get it in the car without me seeing it?* "You can't possibly know someone's pattern of walking. You are perceptive, but you aren't–" Lily's thought ended, and she screamed out loud. A dark figure was tapping on her window.

Gretchen jumped then dug quickly into her bag and grabbed the mace. She turned the flashlight in the direction of the noise. "Lower the window, and I'll spray."

"I didn't know you were armed."

"Lily, roll down the window." Detective Daniel Williams stood next to the car. "Now."

"It's only Daniel."

"Holy Moly, it's Daniel," Lily said as she pushed a button. She smiled up at the man who was dressed in full police gear including his kevlar vest. She was familiar with the outfit, only Dev's said DEA on it. "Hi."

"Hi yourself. Lily, I expect this kind of behavior out of her, but you?"

"She made me do it?" Lily shrugged in defense. Lily eyed Gretchen. "And now you know how it feels to be scared by that tapping on the window."

Gretchen ignored her comment and leaned over to address their intruder. "How did you know we were here? Did you have us followed? I do not appreciate your lack of trust."

Daniel crouched down near the window. "Oh, that's rich, even for you darling. I knew where you were because I placed a tracking device on the rental car. I figured you wouldn't drive your car. You'd want Lily's rental so no one would know who was parked here. You shouldn't be here, and you may have placed our operation in jeopardy."

Gretchen pointed a finger in his direction. "No, you've placed our operation in jeopardy, mister. I'm pretty sure the intruder came in that gap right over there in the hedge. There's just enough room on the fence line to shimmy through." Gretchen pointed the flashlight in the direction.

"And don't you think we know that? Turn that thing off."

"You do?" Gretchen asked as she did as she was instructed.

"Gretchen, Lily go home."

Lily was in the middle of two formidable foes. Literally, she had nowhere to go. "We should go. Thank you, detective."

"Don't thank him," Gretchen growled. "We don't have to go anywhere."

Daniel stood up. "Lily, drive away now, and I won't arrest the two of you for interfering in a police operation."

Lily saluted. "Yes, sir." She hit the ignition and started the car.

"We aren't going anywhere. This is a public street. Turn the car off, Lily."

The woman in the middle glanced at Daniel. His jaw was set. His eyes were thin slits. *I know that look. Dev does the same thing when he has no words to stop me. He just intimidates.* She looked over at her friend. Gretchen's eyes were spitting fire. Even in the dark, she noticed the anger on her face. Her lips were thinly shut.

"You two are placing me in a very bad position. I think you need couple's therapy, not that either of you will go. Detective, we are leaving. Gretchen, be content to know that you had a good idea. Let's leave it for the police."

Lily's window closed. She waved at Daniel and slowly drove down the street, intently heading back to Gretchen's apartment building. Her side glance gave a clear view of a very silent passenger, her arms crossed over her chest.

"I had to, Gretchen."

"The old Lily wouldn't have left. She would've stayed, held the line. You've lost your fighting spirit."

"And I think you pick fights with him to hold him off. Is that what you're doing? You love him. He's told you he loves you, and you've told him, but you are so afraid. Of what? He won't leave you like Chance did. I just feel in my heart he won't."

"Good for you and your little feelings."

But at the end of the block Lily stopped the car. She thought she heard a timid cry from the back seat. When she looked around, Emi was settling herself, her little head leaning against the padding of the carrier. She also noticed a figure all dressed in black getting into a dark colored car opposite the stop sign. "Gretchen, stop pouting and look at that over there."

Gretchen followed Lily's pointing and noticed the innocuous car. "What am I looking at? Our investigation has been thwarted by the law."

"Maybe not," Lily murmured. "Let's follow it."

"Why would we do that?"

Lily heaved a very large, exaggerated sigh. "To placate you, you ninny. And whoever is in that car was coming down the same block we were parked on, and they were dressed all in black. Who in the world does that unless they don't want to be seen?"

Gretchen moistened her lips with a slide of her tongue. "Right. Follow that car."

As the vehicle pulled away, Lily slowly began to drive. She trailed behind as the driver began a trek through The Plaza, heading west across the state line into Kansas.

"Now, this is more like the old days." Gretchen chewed on a snack. She held out a piece of licorice in front of Lily's face. "Licorice?"

Lily happily grabbed the treat and continued to concentrate on the car's path. She'd already placed the license plate to memory, but just in case she was happy to see Gretchen scribbling it down as she held her own treat in her mouth.

"How long do we follow?"

Gretchen thought for a second. "I have no idea. What do you think?"

"I think until that baby in the backseat gets fussy, we drive on. I have a half a tank of gas, and this is the longest I've been out of the house since I was in the hospital on New Year's Eve giving birth."

"You must get a life, bestie."

Lily couldn't roll her eyes, besides Gretchen wouldn't notice anyway. "You think?"

"No wonder you find mysteries all over. You are bored, and I suspect there's days you're overwhelmed and wishing you were arranging flowers in your shop again. By the way, why haven't you visited Abby yet?"

Lily finished chewing her licorice. "Because Abby isn't here. She and Jeremy are on vacation. They're skiing with his parents in Colorado."

"Don't you even want to see the shop?"

Lily slowed down as the car turned right on a side street. "Sure. I'll drive by tomorrow. I might even go in and say hello to Abby's assistant manager. Gretchen, that isn't my life anymore."

Gretchen shook her head in disbelief. "Don't you miss the excitement, the dresses, and the people?"

Lily laughed out loud. "Not really. I coordinate events at Dev's aunts' vineyard, and sometimes the priest needs help with a wedding. I've even arranged flowers for a few weddings and a couple of parties. But, when I made the decision to move to be with Dev, that was it. I never looked back. I have missed Abby and you."

"You're really happy with just Mr. Delicious?"

"You mean with just one man? I've never been like you. You have an appetite for life like no other person I've ever met. For me, Devlin Pierce is everything. We changed each other's lives, for the better."

"Hmmm." Gretchen's silence ushered in a vacuum in the car. The only sound was being emitted from Emi. She remained asleep but was beginning to make a soft noise. *Daniel has filled my life. Have I done the same for him? Of course, I have!*

Lily continued driving, passing shops and streets she used to visit and drive on every week. "Gretchen, do you have any ideas on what's in Mrs. Notte's house that they want so badly to go to such extremes?"

"No, I have no idea."

"You're the super sleuth!"

"Lily, you're the one who took down a terrorist, lives with Mr. Delicious, and is pals with that exotic super-agent Ari."

"My life is very different now." Lily's eyes glanced in the rear-view mirror to see her sleeping daughter.

"Do you think? Don't even get me started about that handsome priest and hunky JT who looks so much like his father." When Gretchen first met the man, she realized she had dated his father many years before. The man had been a captain in the Navy, and they'd shared several nights together. *My, my, my.*

"The car is stopping." Lily's announcement shifted Gretchen's thoughts back to the task at hand. "I'll turn the lights off and hang back."

"We can just sit here all night."

"**We** cannot. I'm going to have to feed Emi pretty soon, and I'll need a bathroom sooner than that."

"You've never had a fortified bladder like mine."

Lily twitched her lips. *If you can't say something nice, just shut up Lily.* "You are one of a kind, that's for sure."

"Thank you." Gretchen removed binoculars from her bag and began to watch.

Lily did a double take. "Are those night vision goggles?"

"No, these are the binoculars. I have the goggles in my bag. I purchased them for a good price at a secondhand store. Do you want to use them?"

Lily turned completely in her seat to view Gretchen Malloy and her newest accessory. "Too bad they aren't in your signature color."

"I know, right?"

Lord, please save me. "Gretchen, the driver is getting out. Hand me the darn goggles."

Gretchen happily reached into the depth of her bag and pulled out the item. "Enjoy."

Lily focused on the dark figure. "That's an apartment building. I had a friend who lived on the second floor. Look, our driver is a woman."

"Yes, it's Diana or whatever her name is. That's Mrs. Notte's dead attorney's assistant."

Lily snapped her fingers. "Andrea, Andrea DiRossi."

Gretchen continued to watch as the young woman walked quickly into building A. "No, Diana Bloome."

"I knew her as Andrea DiRossi," Lily said quietly as she watched the woman.

"How did you know her?"

Lily continued to watch as the woman headed into the building. "She used to work as a photographer's assistant. We met her at several weddings. I think I went out to a bar with her once."

"I'll need to tell Daniel about her double identity," Gretchen murmured.

"No need. He already knows."

Gretchen lowered her binoculars and stared at her supposed friend. "And how do you know that?"

Lily continued to watch the apartment until she saw a light go on just on the second floor as she expected. She lowered the goggles and smiled nervously. Gretchen's glare frightened her like it used to in the old days before their friendship had grown. "I sort of saw some of Daniel's notes after the murder. He had witnesses listed. He had her listed with both names. So, she was the assistant?"

"Yes. In fact, she offered me information on that insurance man who is actually a fence."

"And what is his name? Do you remember?"

Gretchen lowered the binoculars. "Well, of course I do. Lily, you keep forgetting that I am a professional. I remember and know every important detail."

Except now that Diana Bloome is really Andrea DiRossi. "So, what is his name?"

"The name on his card was Ross D'Angelo. He worked for West Expansion Insurance Company, and the address was for a corporate building in San Francisco. I checked, and it was legitimate, but they never heard of Ross D'Angelo."

"Ross D'Angelo and Andrea DiRossi? I bet they're related."

"No, Lily. She insisted there was something wrong with the insurance man. She thought I should check him out."

"Uh huh. Why would she be hanging out on the street with the back entrance to Mrs. Notte's property on a night when she knew the house would be unattended?"

"She played me. She's involved. But why? Was it really just a money scheme?"

"It probably was always for the money and the jewelry, but what is in that house that they want their hands on? Why do they want the property sold?"

"There has to be something, maybe buried treasure?"

Lily grimaced. She touched her breasts. "Okay, this sleuthing is over for tonight. I need to get back to your place and feed her."

"Can't that wait? The dear little girl isn't even fussing yet."

"My boobs tell me I need to feed her real soon, and that usually means she'll begin wailing any minute now."

Gretchen clicked her tongue against the top of her mouth. "Children are very needy. No wonder I never had time for them."

"Well, you do need to make time for them. You have to feed them, clean them, and make sure they sleep the required hours." Lily had already begun to turn around. "You very rarely wear heels when you have them either."

"That's inexcusable and bridges on the precipice of insanity."

Heels and insane…that goes together, and the photo for an example would be my bestie Gretchen Malloy!

Chapter Sixteen

Lily nursed her one and only glass of wine for the evening while Gretchen poured her second glass full. After their adventure and a feeding, Emi was asleep for at least a few hours. As they heard the doorknob turn, they remained still and silent. The detective was home.

Daniel entered to see the faces of two beguiling women smiling widely at him. It was unnerving. He was tired; he was disappointed. "Ladies." As he removed his jacket and threw his keys on the kitchen island, he looked from Lily to Gretchen. "It's too late for this. What the hell is going on?"

Gretchen moved with the speed of a ninja and presented him with his favorite beer. "Go sit down. Relax. You must be tired after that long stakeout."

"It's still ongoing," Daniel grumbled. "Jerry took over." He collapsed in the chair opposite Lily's position on the couch. "I suppose we won't discuss what happened earlier?"

Lily looked down in her wine glass and her companion ignored his question completely. "So, darling Daniel we have information for you," Gretchen began as she sashayed back to the couch and Lily's side.

Daniel shut his eyes. He seemed to be mumbling something about dumpster diving, but Gretchen ignored him.

"Lily and I have discovered that the attorney's assistant, Diana/Andrea is in on the whole thing."

"Yes."

Lily nudged Gretchen. "What does that mean?"

"In Daniel speak that means he probably knew or suspected that already, but he doesn't know she was at the house tonight. We saw her. She was dressed all in black."

"Yes."

Gretchen nudged Lily. "He already knew that too. Well, he is a very good detective."

"Ladies, I'm too tired for this. What don't I know?"

"Andrea DiRossi is related to the insurance fence guy, Ross D'Angelo. I had Dev run a check," Lily said proudly.

Daniel rubbed his forehead. "Dev ran a check for you. Wonderful," he murmured.

Lily smirked. "You know him by a couple of other names, including Nathan and Buddy. But Ross is a well-known Miami fence. You and Dev already knew that, but what you didn't know is that Andrea is his niece. The two of them have been running scams and thefts for over a year here in Kansas City. Mrs. Notte's attorney was getting some cash here and there, but the majority of his payback was in jewelry. Another insurance company was investigating the attorney about an antique armoire and another necklace made of opals."

Gretchen softly landed her hand on Lily's leg. "Opals can be bad luck. I guess it was for him. Tell Daniel the really big news."

Daniel took a long drink from his beer bottle. "Oh, please do."

Lily enthusiastically answered. "Andrea DiRossi used to receive flower deliveries through my shop several years ago. She worked for a photographer part time, worked as a waitress while she was going to law school. I didn't remember until an hour ago that she was dating a client of mine…Garrett Notte."

Daniel nearly spat out his drink. "No way."

"I'm going to the shop tomorrow to confirm. The information should still be in the computer history."

Daniel pushed up to the edge of the chair. "Is Garrett manipulating all of this?"

"We're not sure," Gretchen offered. "I'm not sure we can know for sure. If someone were to ask him, he could lie or he might be tipped off. If Andrea is going after something big in that house, Garrett might not know."

"Daniel, I think he may have said something, and she remembered the information," Lily added. "Her uncle and she are going after a big payoff. We just can't figure out what it might be."

Daniel leaned back in the chair. "Has anyone ever asked Mrs. Notte if there's something hidden in the house or on the grounds of the house? If it were sold, there would be an opportunity to grab whatever it is."

Gretchen and Lily blinked at each other. "Well that makes sense, doesn't it?"

Gretchen nodded. "He is rather remarkable, isn't he?"

"Oh yeah, remarkable. That's me. I have two amateur sleuths holding a stakeout while I'm trying to draw out a criminal or two." Daniel stopped, looking directly in their direction. His voice raised. "And you had a baby in the backseat! Again, what were you two thinking?"

Lily bowed her head. "We weren't. We wanted to help."

"No, it's my fault. I lured Lily to the site. She had no idea," Gretchen admitted.

"I figured you were serious when you pulled out those night vision–"

Daniel shot out of the chair. "**You** have night vision binoculars?"

Gretchen nodded enthusiastically. "Of course, and I have goggles too. I'm a professional. I have the equipment I need."

Lily snorted. *Gretchen certainly has equipment! She might be annoying, but Gretchen Malloy is certainly entertaining. I'll have stories for Dev for hours after this trip.*

Daniel finished his bottle of beer in another drink. "It's late. I need to get some sleep before I hit it again tomorrow."

Upon his pronouncement, Gretchen and Lily watched him rise from the chair, place his bottle on the kitchen island and head over to his keys and coat.

Gretchen shot up off of the couch. She tapped her foot, for once her heels did not emit one sound on the rug. "Daniel!"

"What?"

"Do not go out that door!"

Lily watched as though she was the daughter in the middle of daddy and mommy's argument. On the other hand, she was mildly entertained that Gretchen didn't always get her way when it came to this man.

"I'm going to my own bed, to sleep. I'm tired of all of your, your antics." The detective's hand reached for the knob.

"You leave, and you do not come back. Do you understand?"

Lily gulped as she looked up at Gretchen's face. *She's pushing him away. If she does that she'll have more time to call me, and she'll complain...a lot! I can't allow that to happen.* "Gretchen, don't utter the ultimatum. It doesn't work with men like him. I know that for a fact," Lily said quietly.

Gretchen looked down at her friend. "But I have to, Lily."

"Nope. You do not have to, Gretchen. You just don't like him being the one who is doing the leaving. We've talked about this."

As the ladies discussed, Daniel turned the knob and opened the door. "Gretchen, I love you, but I have to leave. I'll see you both in the morning. Lily, I'd like to go with you to the flower shop, if you don't mind."

"Yes, that would be a good idea. I should be ready by nine."

Daniel nodded. "I'll see you then. I'll bring **her** favorite pastries." He began to walk into the hallway but turned back around. He seemed to be having an internal battle of some kind. Briskly stepping back into the apartment, Daniel acted before thinking. He grabbed Gretchen in his arms and kissed her senseless. Once he was done with her, Daniel released his hold. Gretchen took a slight step backwards as she collected her balance, her breath, and even her thoughts.

He looked back at the door. "Gretchen, you make me lose my mind despite the fact I love you. But don't you ever give me an ultimatum like that again. I'll see you in the morning, darling."

The door closed. It seemed as if all of the oxygen had been sucked out of the room by some sort of a controlled burn named Daniel Williams. Lily and Gretchen blinked at each other. Lily finished off her glass of wine in a toast to a man who just made her friend speechless.

As Gretchen dropped down onto the couch, she grabbed her own glass and took a swig. "What the hell just happened?"

Lily smiled. "I believe I just witnessed the besting of Gretchen Malloy. You will let him in tomorrow morning, won't you?"

Gretchen was befuddled, confused, and every other word that described utter surprise. "What?"

"You will let him in. I'd like those pastries. Weren't your favorites from that French bakery…"

Gretchen had no idea what Lily was babbling about. *What is she saying? What did Daniel say? The man disregarded my threat and added his own. That man! Who did he think he was? What should I do?*

"Gretchen?"

Gretchen faced Lily. "Lily, I love him so much. I don't want to live a life without him. That frightens me."

Lily tenderly removed the wine glass from Gretchen's hands and then took them into her own. "I'm so happy for you. Love is frightening, but now that you have it in your life, you have to fight to keep it. And let him bring those pastries!"

"Sure."

Lily noticed her friend's eyes filling with tears. "Gretchen? Is the once powerful and all-consuming Ms. Malloy having her heart beat again? You've let him in. You've let me, Dev, and the kids in. Oh my gosh, you might actually become a real human being."

Gretchen wiped her eyes. "Don't push it. If I do become a normal human, I'm still wearing fabulous heels."

"Of course. I wouldn't expect anything less from you. Did I see cheesecake in the refrigerator?"

Gretchen straightened her back and sniffed back the tears. "Yes, and I made it. It has a caramel drizzle on top with pecans. I'm cutting two big pieces."

Lily watched as Gretchen headed into the kitchen. The heels clicked on the floor. "Daniel, you are all powerful if you're the reason the great Gretchen Malloy's heart is beating and full of life."

Gretchen looked up at her friend. "Did you say something, Lily?"

"I was wondering if I might have just a teensy more wine?" Lily lied.

Gretchen's smile was larger than usual. "Of course. I'm so happy I've finally corrupted you! It's nice to have the old Lily back."

But you aren't the old Gretchen I left behind, and that makes me happy.

Chapter Seventeen

"Exactly how did you and Gretchen become friends?" Daniel asked as he drove down Wornall Road into the Brookside area of Kansas City.

Lily laughed. "Truthfully, I still don't know, and there are those days when I'm not sure I want to be. Do you think she can handle Emi for an hour?"

"We'll get the info and get back as soon as we can. I understand those days when you're not sure. Last night–"

"You stood your ground. She needs that," Lily stated flatly. "She's been on her own for so long, she needs to take baby steps even in those stilettos."

"I've learned that if I give her an inch, she'll take a foot."

"Or two feet, a yard, well she'll pretty much take the entire football field," Lily added. "Daniel, you can park in that lot on the left."

As they walked up to Lily's Flower Shop, the homecoming brought back memories for one of the visitors. As they came near the door, Lily looked down at the pavement. John, her dear friend, had been shot in the doorway as he protected her. This was the location where Garrett had threatened her, and this was the place where a handsome DEA agent had walked into the shop and changed her life forever.

Daniel noticed some hesitation in Lily. "Are you okay?"

"Yes, just thinking about how it used to be."

Daniel opened the door for Lily to enter. She saw the same table near the front of the shop where she usually conducted consultations with her many brides. The front window had a lovely display of spring flowers with a large wreath created from fake birds. *Interesting, and it has Abby's name written all over it.*

"Good morning." A young woman approached them before they stood in the middle of the shop. She looked at Lily and smiled. "You're Lily, aren't you?"

"Yes, and you're Robin. Abby has told me so much about you. It's so nice to meet you."

"You know she's out of town, right? She'll be back on Sunday. Will you be here?"

"Sadly, no. Robin, this is Detective Daniel Williams with the KCPD, and I was wondering if I could, or if you could look up a past client history. It should still be in the system. The detective needs some information."

Robin moved in the direction of the counter where the computer system was still housed. "What's the name?"

"Notte. There should be two or three files, but we want the one for Garrett."

Robin hit a few buttons while they waited. Daniel looked around. "Lily, this is a nice shop. Was it hard to leave?"

"I was discussing that with Gretchen. Once I made the decision, I knew where my future would be. It was with Dev in Virginia. Maybe one day we'll move back, but it will be years."

"Lily, would you like to see the file?"

Daniel and the former owner came behind the counter. Lily scrolled the file. "Here it is, Daniel. I was right." Leaning over Lily's shoulder, Williams shot a photo of the screen. "I'll email me a copy, and I can send it to you. I might as well send a copy of Mrs. Notte's and Bernard's invoices too. Robin?"

"Go ahead. I know Mrs. Notte. She's a nice lady. She had Abby and me in for tea when we decorated the house for Christmas."

"Yes, she is lovely." *And she was a kleptomaniac when she came into the shop. Barrett used to come in a day later and pay us.* Lily found all the information and forwarded it to her email account. "Well, that's what we needed. Thank you, Robin. I'll call Abby next week."

"It was so nice meeting you both."

They were leaving the shop when Robin stopped them. "Lily, did you say the name Gretchen a little bit ago? Is that Gretchen Malloy?"

Lily giggled. She could only imagine what Robin thought of the woman who used to send chills down her spine. "Yes, what has she done to you?"

"She just scares me. I broke out in hives while decorating an arbor last fall. She was standing there analyzing every bloom, every move I made. I couldn't make her happy."

Daniel and Lily shared a knowing look. The detective patted the assistant manager on the shoulder. "Don't worry, the best of us can't make her happy. Thanks for your help, Robin."

Once in the car, the two laughed out loud. Lily took a breath. "Well, Gretchen still has it!"

"She used to, and sometimes still can, give me a headache," Daniel admitted. "Do we have time?"

"Sure, what's up?"

Daniel opened the car door and looked back at Lily. "I need to order flowers. I'll be right back."

Alone in the car, Lily shook her head. "God bless you, Detective Williams. What a man you are!" She pulled her phone from her purse and pressed Dev's number. "Hello honey. I miss you."

"I miss you. Your son has been sleeping with me in our bed. He's not a snuggler like his mother, but he does kick. Lily, I have a meeting in two minutes."

"Go, I just wanted to hear your voice. I love you. Maybe we can talk tonight?"

She could hear Dev gathering papers on his desk. "Sure, tonight. Love you too. Tell Daniel hello, and Gretchen, tell her to behave."

"And she'll say to behave like what, or where's the fun in that?"

"Oh my Lord, you've been there too long. You can quote her. Get home. Bye, honey."

"I can do more than quote her, Mr. Delicious." They hung up in laughter.

Chapter Eighteen

Lily reminded Daniel to remove the tracker from her rental car as he dropped her back at the apartment. Hopefully, she could see Mrs. Notte one more time and drive by all of her favorite places. Tonight, she'd pack for the flight tomorrow.

As she entered the apartment, she began to yell out a robust hello, but instead slowly crept in. Gretchen was asleep on the couch, sitting up with Emi sleeping soundly on her chest. Lily removed her phone and shot a quick photo. *This is probably the most motherly Gretchen has ever been, and I want proof. Even if she told Dev, he wouldn't believe her without a clear piece of evidence. And I can use it for blackmail someday.*

The aroma from the kitchen told her that Gretchen had been cooking. Lily checked the stove and lowered the heat. She then took the quiet time to pack up a few things before she heard Emi's light cries. Lily stopped in the hallway.

"Emi, we discussed this behavior. Auntie G doesn't like it when you sound so disagreeable. Auntie G prefers you display your angelic personality. No one likes criers. You need to be strong, even strong-willed. Oh, Daddy and Mommy won't like it, but you'll be highly entertaining to me. Always know that I love you and your brother very much. Never doubt that."

Lily's hand went up to her mouth at the sight. She watched in awe as Gretchen nuzzled Emi's little nose. Emi had actually quieted. "Hi."

Gretchen was surprised at her presence. "When did you get back?"

"While Emi and you were taking your little nap, Auntie G."

As soon as Lily rounded the couch, Gretchen handed the baby off to her mother. "My arms were getting sore. How did it go at the shop?"

"Robin is very nice, and yes, I remembered correctly. We copied all of the files on every Notte order since we began that computer system. Garrett did send flowers to Andrea several years ago. He was probably in college or just out when he began. I guess they were dating."

Gretchen's eyebrow rose. "Maybe he was just thanking her for something?"

"Your mind always goes in the gutter, doesn't it?" Lily reprimanded.

"Absolutely not. Perhaps it slides into a ditch on occasion, but never a gutter. How about lunch? I have a pot of soup on the stove. Emi and I made it while you were off with that detective."

Gretchen had already walked into the kitchen. "That detective is the great love of your life." Lily snuggled her baby. "Your Auntie G doesn't know how good she has it."

"Do not lie to your baby. I know exactly how wonderful my life is because I created it," Gretchen said defiantly. "Me."

Lily turned around to look at her friend. "Ah, so you're afraid you'll lose control."

"Yes, no. I have no idea what you're talking about, Lily." Gretchen continued to pull two bowls from the cabinet. She set out placemats at the island, grabbed two spoons, and began to serve lunch. "Are you ready to eat?"

"Let me lay her down, and I'll be right back." Emi's eyes were already heavy. She'd be back to sleep as soon as Lily walked out of the room.

Before Lily could even eat her soup, there was a knock at the door. "I'll get it." She wasn't surprised by the doorman's delivery. "I'll give it to her. Thank you."

"What in the world was that, Lily?"

"This." Lily's face and half of her body was blocked from Gretchen's view by a large vase of elegant orchid strands.

Gretchen's spoon hit the counter with a thump. "Oh my."

"That's an understatement. There's phalaenopsis, cymbidiums, dendrobiums, and oncidiums," Lily explained.

"You forgot the cattleyas. I haven't seen such beautiful orchids since–"

Lily placed the vase of exotics on the kitchen island. "Yes?"

Gretchen's shoulders dropped. Daniel's home on the island had been filled with orchids when they arrived, and all of them were just for her. She leaned against the counter as she surveyed her gift. She began to cry. "He is a dear man, isn't he?"

"In the old days, before I really knew you, I'd say you really didn't deserve Daniel Williams. But, Gretchen, you're what I would call sassy. You say things I would never dream of having come out of my mouth. I understand how you seize life. I envy you for that ability. Now, seize the love you deserve, and don't ever look back. You deserve the best, always."

Gretchen merely nodded. She sniffed back the tears and shook her head to compose herself. "Sit down and eat your soup before it gets cold."

"And then I'd like to visit Mrs. Notte one more time this afternoon."

"I'll give her one of my beautiful orchids. You know they are my signature flowers."

The soup was good. Lily looked up and winked. "Apparently, someone else knows that too."

Gretchen nearly threw the spoon at her friend. She knew she was defeated. "Fine. I love Daniel. I love him so much I want him to get rid of that pathetic little apartment he has. I will give him more than one shelf. I'll give him part of my closet to hang his suits. I'll–"

"Yes?" Lily watched suspiciously as Gretchen listed her declarations. "Do you need post-it notes, or maybe we should get you a white board like I have so you could write them down and erase them as you fulfill the job?"

"I don't need your blasted white board or those post-it notes! I can keep more than one thing in my head."

"And the most important thing?"

Gretchen bowed her head. "I need to tell him I want a future with him, don't I?"

"And you won't wiggle out of it. You will not suggest he deserves someone who can give him kids. You will be content knowing he knows what he wants, and God help him, it is you."

When Gretchen looked up she had doubts. "His mother is only a few years older than me. Also, why should loving me prevent him from having a child of his own?"

Lily shook her head. "You don't get it. He wants a life with you. I'm sure he'd love a child, but people do live without them, and they do it very happily." Lily swirled her spoon in the bowl. "You could let him get someone pregnant and raise the child as your own."

Lily heard the stamping of the heels on the wood floor. "Lily Pierce, bite your tongue. **That** will not be happening!"

"You could suggest it to Daniel–"

"Stop it. You are just goading me. Fine, I'll ask him."

Lily dropped her spoon, sending a bit of liquid onto the counter. "You love him so much you'd do that?"

With Gretchen's slight nod, Lily smiled. "Holy Moly, Gretchen. You've become a full-fledged human being with a real heart."

Gretchen straightened her form and lifted her chin. "Believe me, it is highly overrated."

And she's back! Lily ate her lunch and was secure knowing she wouldn't be losing hours of time in nightly phone calls with a lovelorn Gretchen. The woman would be just fine.

Chapter Nineteen

The next morning, the door man had Lily's rental parked in the driveway and her luggage in the trunk. He knocked at the door one final time.

Lily ran to let the poor man in. She'd taken enough of his time today. He seemed out of place. She blinked. He blinked.

"Mrs. Pierce, I removed your shovel. I don't think you want to take that on the plane, do you?"

Lily turned slowly around and stared at Gretchen. Her heels tapped quickly on the wood floor. She laughed oddly. "Oh, there it is. That's mine. So sorry. Thank you. We'll be downstairs in just a few minutes."

With the closing of the door, Gretchen knew she'd turn to see a confused Lily. But she didn't. The simple former florist had her arms crossed and her face seemed a little flushed.

"Gretchen, you had that small one in your bag, but did you also have that in the trunk for the stake out?"

"Of course." Gretchen walked briskly past her and placed the shovel in the broom closet. "You never know when you might need to dig up something, or in your case, someone. Don't pretend to be lily white when it comes to investigations and murder." Gretchen giggled.

"Lily white! Sometimes I surprise myself with my brilliance."

"Keep telling yourself that," Lily mumbled. She looked around the living room. "I've already checked your guest room twice. I have everything packed. All I need is Emi, my carryon, and my purse." Lily picked up the car keys. Her stomach was churning. The trip here wasn't too bad, but they had left early in the morning. The late afternoon flight worried her, not to mention going through TSA was a challenge. Surrendering her concerns didn't seem to be practical. She just needed to see them all as challenges she could overcome in order to see her son and husband again. Leaving Gretchen was equally difficult. "Thank you for having us. I wasn't sure, but–"

Gretchen bounded toward her and embraced her tightly. "Make Dev move here."

Lily's eyes teared up. "I can't do that. We have plans." Lily pulled away and patted her eyes. "And you should too. That entire discussion we had about the children...I figured it all out. It's more about you and less about Daniel. You're suddenly having regrets after all of these years about not having your own children, your own family. My, the great Malloy has fallen."

Gretchen firmly shut her eyes. "I have. Daniel has made me think about what could've been if we'd just met earlier."

"You can't think like that. I didn't think I'd have the family or the man, and one day he just walked into my shop."

"Daniel arrested me, then arrested me again when he caught me in that dumpster."

Lily shook her head. *Where is Abby when I need her? She'd mumble something about dumpster diving in those heels.* "You meet the best people at the worst times, Auntie G."

Gretchen glanced at the sleeping baby. "May I borrow your children in a few years, after they are potty trained?"

"Of course, but with adult supervision." Lily laughed at her own joke while she placed the purse on her shoulder and grabbed the carrier. "Could you grab the carryon?"

"Sure."

The elevator ride down to the car happened in complete silence. The door man grabbed Lily's carryon and helped her insert Emi's carrier into the car seat. Lily was closing the door softly when Daniel arrived.

"I thought I'd miss you. Have a good flight. I'm sure your husband and son miss you." Daniel strode up to Lily and gave her a quick hug. "It was so nice meeting you Lily."

"I enjoyed your company, Daniel." Lily reached up to whisper. "Take care of our girl."

"I will most definitely."

Gretchen came over for one final hug and to look through the window at Emi. "I still don't want you to go."

"If I don't go, I can't come back."

Gretchen pursed her lips as though she'd tasted something unsavory. "That is the most ridiculous thing I've ever heard, but you're right. Go, so you can come back again." Daniel slipped his arm around her waist.

As Lily entered the car, she asked one final question. "And you two will catch whoever is doing this to Mrs. Notte, right?"

Gretchen glanced at Daniel. Daniel looked at Gretchen. They both nodded. "We will catch them, Lily. I'm sure she'll update you by the end of the week. I have a plan."

Gretchen clapped. "I love it when he has a plan. We went to the Bahamas the last time."

Lily chuckled. "Good luck, Daniel. You'll need all of it you can muster with this one. Gretchen, I'll text or call tonight after we land. I love you."

Gretchen bit her lip but it was of no avail. She began blubbering like a baby. "You know I haven't had a sister here with me in a very long time."

"I know, but I'm just a phone call away."

"I love you too, Lily."

Lily's heart couldn't take it anymore. She closed the door and drove slowly away. She brushed back her own tears and took one final look to see Gretchen and Daniel walking into the building hand-in-hand.

"Holy Moly! I just became her stand-in sister? After all of those years she put me through? Well, maybe that was just purgatory, and I'm in heaven now? Devlin is not going to believe this, and Abby is going to think I've gone mad."

In the rear-view mirror, she saw a sleeping baby. "Emi, let's go home."

Chapter Twenty

"Daniel, I've been thinking about little Andrea and her beau Garrett Notte," Gretchen said as she poured her detective a cup of coffee. "Do you want a sandwich with that? I have turkey or ham."

"Turkey would be fine." Daniel sat at the island. He looked around the living area. It was quiet. It seemed untouched. "I'm going to miss Lily and Emi."

Gretchen prepared his food, adding his favorite dill pickles and a little brown mustard. "I don't want to talk about them. I want to talk about the criminals."

"Lily makes you do a lot of soul searching, doesn't she?"

"She's a pest."

Daniel laughed out loud. "You don't mean that. She's the closest to you since Amy, right? You let her in. I bet you didn't even want to do that, but it just happened." Daniel patted himself on the back. "Kind of like me?"

Gretchen's bottom lip quivered. *What spell has Lily placed on me? I don't want to be just like every other human being. I'm Gretchen Malloy, but I can't seem to help it.* "Daniel, I love you very much. I want you to move in with me, to share this beautiful apartment. I won't give it up, and I won't give up on you. We could adopt if you really want a family. We'll have to hire a nanny. I won't be participating in those ridiculous mommy-child track and field events. Although, even in stilettos I could beat those women."

Daniel came over to the unusually frazzled woman in heels and took her in his arms. "My lease is up in June. I'll need more than just one drawer, and I'll need a place for my sports gear."

"There's a storage unit in the basement."

"Perfect. G, look at me." He tilted her chin up. It hurt his heart to see the always in-control woman crying. "I'm good with spoiling Emi."

"And little Drew is an absolute angel. You will adore him."

"Then, you're stuck with me, Gretchen Malloy, come hell or broken heel."

Gretchen wrapped her arms around her detective and kissed him soundly. "If you purchase a really good pair of stilettos, you hardly ever break a heel, silly man. Thank you for loving me. I didn't know I needed you."

"And I certainly didn't know I needed you. We're the perfect couple."

"It seems that way. Now, eat your sandwich and tell me about Andrea."

Daniel did as he was told, but there wasn't much to tell. "So, she knew Garrett, and she's the niece of the fraudulent insurance agent/fence."

Gretchen held a finger in the air. "But she and Garrett were more than friends. Lily and I went back through her retail files. He wrote sweet things on the notes at first. Then Garrett became a little dark. It was very weird even for someone like Mrs. Notte's criminal grandson.

Daniel wiped the mustard off the side of his mouth. "How dark?"

"Things like meeting her on street corners. He threatened to bring her sweetness with her. It's kinky, but there was such a quick turn in those notes."

Daniel's gray eyes held a spark. "May I see them?"

"Sure. I downloaded them on my computer so we wouldn't have to bother Lily all the time. I have all the files from the Notte family."

Gretchen pulled her laptop to the kitchen island and soon had the files of information for Daniel to review. She watched him scan file after file. He quickly ran through Mrs. Notte's. He spent more time on Bernard's, but his attention was intense while he read Garrett's orders. He pointed at one note in particular.

"The notes changed because their relationship changed. Look at this…he liked her. He wanted a romantic hookup."

"Hookup doesn't sound right coming out of your mouth," Gretchen scolded. "You're more of a making love, rendezvous kind of man, Daniel. Maybe a tryst?"

Daniel's lips formed a thin smile. He liked the sound of a tryst. "I'll never say it again. Then look about three months in, they begin setting up these meetings." Daniel grabbed his phone and began to input addresses. "Gretchen, they were selling drugs. This corner is notorious for dealers; this other address is the prime area to pick up crack, meth, anything you want. Considering this was several years ago, those areas are still known for drug trafficking."

"Perhaps Garrett was her dealer, not her lover?"

"Perhaps, Andrea was his entry into the drug world."

Gretchen mulled Daniel's climatic hypothesis. "That would be interesting. He had to get into that hell somehow. He didn't just go up to the tennis pro at the country club and tell him he wanted to be a world renown cartel king, did he?"

Daniel cocked his head to the side. "Can you get me into the club?"

Gretchen stood proudly, her hands on her ample hips. "Honey, I can get you in anywhere in this city, and if they were to see your bank account, you could get yourself in all on your little own."

"Good." He looked down at his watch. "I've got to get going. Dinner later?" He kissed her quickly before making his way to the door.

"Yes, I'll cook. I feel sad so I'll bake."

"Good." Daniel was in the hallway when Gretchen remembered a date.

"Daniel, they have an open membership event Saturday night at the club. Would you like to go? Maybe you could be yourself and not the detective?"

"I can do that once in a while, darling. I'll even bring my checkbook, the real one. See you later." The elevator door opened, he waved goodbye, and vanished.

Gretchen danced a few salsa steps in celebration. "I'm going to the club with the real Mr. Daniel Williams, Esquire from Boston, Massachusetts. Woohoo! What shall I wear?"

Chapter Twenty-One

"You seem nervous, and the great Gretchen Malloy is never nervous," Daniel chided as the valet took his car keys, and they began their triumphant entrance into one of the most prestigious country clubs in the city.

"I've never gone to one of these events with a very rich man on my arm."

"You're on **my** arm." He patted her hand at the crook of his elbow.

"Logistics are not important as long as we end up at the correct location. Everyone will see us. I think Marty will be here tonight."

"The senator? Wonderful. I seem to like all of your friends."

Gretchen placed her fake smile on her face and spoke through her teeth. "Even Chance?"

"Chance wasn't your friend. He was your ex. There's a big difference."

Gretchen noticed the low tone, the lustful glance. *Oh my! You can be a jealous one, Daniel!* "Difference noted. We check in here." She noticed a couple of club workers she knew from past parties. They offered the work required pleasantries and sent them on their way.

As they entered the larger room of the club, Gretchen was hailed by several of her former clients. She nodded in their direction but remained at Daniel's side.

"You seem very popular," Daniel commented. He steered them toward the nearest bar.

"I'm only popular because I'm with the most handsome and mysterious man here." She grabbed his arm tightly. If she had to fight off the women she was prepared with a mini mace in her purse and several hat pins that although weren't technically used these days, came in very handy while warding off handsy females and the occasional drunken flirt.

"What are you drinking tonight?"

"What are you drinking?"

"I'll have a classic martini." She pointed at the bartender. "Daniel, this is Orly Fontaine, and he is the best bartender in the entire city. Orly has worked at this club for over twenty years. He knows everyone, everything, and anything that needs to be known."

The elderly man offered a toothy smile. "Ms. Malloy knows things too. Don't let her fool you. One classic martini for the prettiest lady here in heels coming right up."

"And for you, dear Daniel?"

"Orly, surprise me." Daniel leaned on the side of the bar. He looked like he owned the place and was bored with the festivities.

"You are a natural in this environment. How did you fool me?" Gretchen whispered.

"You weren't watching back then."

"I was, but I was usually just watching you walk away. You have a lovely backside."

Daniel shook his head. No other woman could make him blush and lust at the same time.

Orly presented the perfect martini to Gretchen and looked over at her companion. "Is he yours now, Ms. Malloy?"

"He is. This is Daniel Williams. His family owns a diamond company, an over a century old one."

"Then, I believe I will fix you a Vesper martini. That's what a certain super agent by the name of James drinks."

Daniel glanced at Gretchen. "Then serve it up. A super agent is exactly what I am."

"We could play at that later, Jimmy," Gretchen purred. "Oh, I see Marty."

"Go on. I'll catch up. Besides, I'd like to pick Orly's memory bank."

Gretchen thought she heard a rumor about a very wealthy diamond merchant as she meandered through the guests. With this crowd the stories flew fast around the room. "I've missed you," she announced as she stood in Marty's path. "How are you, Senator?"

"I'm fine now that you're here, Ms. Malloy. Put that drink down and give me a proper greeting." The new U.S. Senator beckoned her with open arms.

Gretchen placed her martini carefully on the nearest table and stepped into the warm embrace. "You seem to still be alive and well," she whispered in his ear.

Marty kissed her and stepped back. Gretchen grabbed her very tasty drink. "I'm surprised to see you here, Gretchen. Are you going to join the club for real this time?"

Gretchen smirked. "Why exactly should I? I can get a visitor's pass anytime I really need one. I still send more brides to the club than any other planner, and they know how valuable I am to have around." She pointed over to the bar and noticed Orly and Daniel in a head-to-head discussion. "I'm here with Daniel. He's thinking of joining."

"Really? On a police detective's salary?"

"Not exactly. Daniel is the sole heir to a very world renowned company that has a legacy of millions of dollars. He may join the club."

Marty slapped his leg. "You knew he had money, didn't you? Is that why you chose him over Chance?"

Suddenly, Gretchen fell ill. "How dare you think I'm that shallow! I didn't know, and he chose me. Chance never did that. He never placed me first, remember?"

"Whoa, simmer down. I'm sorry. I didn't know. I apologize."

"You should. I'm touchy about Daniel's star being diminished by opinions like yours. This man picked our community. He chose to serve. That's very admirable."

Marty agreed. "Very admirable and commendable. But you have to admit you are one lucky woman."

Gretchen glanced back at her detective one more time. "You have no idea how lucky I am. He loves me."

"Are you two going to marry?"

Gretchen took a sip of her martini and smiled. "I have no idea. We're happy. That's enough for now."

Marty understood. "That is enough. Just be happy. And I'm very happy for you. He's a good man, even if he does have money."

"Snob!"

"Obstinate."

"Well, I suppose I am in some cases, but I can be very flexible." Before Marty could continue with a witty retort, Daniel Williams took Gretchen's side, kissing her before he greeted the senator.

"She is flexible," Daniel added. "Good to see you again, Senator."

"And good to see you. I hear you have stolen my friend's heart."

Gretchen huffed. "He didn't steal it. I gave it freely, and do not make a joke about how free I can be."

Marty pretended to be locking his lips. "I wouldn't think of it. So, Williams, will you be joining the club?"

"I'm not sure if I have the time for it. Between my work and volunteer projects, it doesn't leave me a lot of room to just come to the club. I've never gotten into golf. I swim and play tennis, but neither are that important to me."

"What do you like?" Marty asked.

"Boxing. I box."

"Really? Amazing. Have you ever thought of being part of a security detail? Like mine?"

"Frankly, Senator, I haven't. I'm content on the force here in this great city. Kansas City is my home now, and so is this woman." Daniel moved his arm protectively around Gretchen's waist. "Unless she wants to move."

Gretchen's body molded into his. "I don't. That was a wonderful offer, Marty, but Daniel and I are staying put for now."

Marty patted Gretchen's arm. "I just saw a congressman I need to speak with about a house bill. I'll be here until next Wednesday. Can we all get together?"

Gretchen and Daniel nodded and allowed the man to take care of his business. Before Marty had even met up with his political peer, Gretchen wanted to know what Daniel had discovered.

"What did Orly tell you?"

Daniel's gray eyes were twinkling. "First, he makes the best martini I have ever had, and second, he knows everything. You were right."

"So, tell me before that woman over there comes here and bothers us. She's part of the membership committee, and she's probably already run a check on you, found your history online, and has calculated how much you're worth."

"Then let's find a quiet corner."

Gretchen grabbed his hand and began to steer him through the crowd. "I know the perfect place." Away from the crowd, she directed him down a quiet hallway. At the end of the path was a secluded corner which held a table and lamp in the middle of two chairs.

"This is nice."

Gretchen agreed. "It's my place when I have a wedding or event here. I take my shoes off and put my feet up. The kitchen is on the other side of that door over there, I grab a plate of food, and just take a break."

"I like it here. It's cozy."

"Yes, yes, now tell me what you found out. Stay on task, Daniel."

"Yes, ma–Gretchen. Orly knew Garrett very well, his dad, and grandparents too. You knew the grandfather had his own financial difficulties. It seems like Mrs. Notte has rebuilt the fortune. But for Garrett and Bernard it was never enough. They didn't want to work. They just wanted the money."

"That's very true. Nepotism and trust funds seem to corrupt even the best of people, present company excepted."

"Thanks for that. Little Andrea came with Garrett to the club a lot. Did you know he purchased an associate membership for her? She came without him then and was very close with the tennis pro."

"Oh, him." Gretchen rolled her eyes. "If you think my ego is large, you should see his. It's the size of Saturn, the planet!"

"We are speaking about his ego, right? Or do you need to tell me something about you and–"

Gretchen slapped playfully at Daniel's sleeve. "Never him. There's something about him I never liked."

"Well, I ran a quick check on him. Did you know he's been busted for illegal possession of narcotics, mostly substitutes for prescription painkillers?"

Gretchen twisted her lips in thought. "Yet he still works at the club?"

"Yes, and he just jumped to the top of my list of suspects. If you turn very carefully and look out the window to the other side of the patio, you'll see him with Andrea."

"And that is the key, Daniel. So, all of this is related, and it goes back to Garrett Notté, but what is in that house that they want so badly? Lily and I had no clues."

"Or somewhere on the property?"

Gretchen nodded in agreement. "That would make sense if they want the property, not just the house. Let's say this is all about Garrett and his drug deals."

"Maybe he left information there that Mrs. Notte knows nothing about as some sort of an insurance policy?" Daniel watched the tennis pro and the attorney's assistant carefully. Obviously, the two were together in some form. How and why they were together was the million dollar question.

"We should get Mrs. Notte flowers and visit her tomorrow at the rehab center. You'd be a wonderful diversion for her despair."

"Despair?"

Gretchen patted his hand. "She's finished, at least she thinks that. I won't be finished until I take my last breath. There will always be something to plan, somewhere to go."

Daniel leaned over and kissed her cheek. He allowed his hand to tenderly slide down the side of her face to eventually rest on her shoulder. "With you, there's always something, and that is a very good thing."

"Sweet man," Gretchen whispered as she leaned into his caress. She turned back around to view their suspects once more. "Daniel, I think I should go over there and have a small discussion."

"Um, no. I do not think you should do that."

"Don't be a stick in the mud. Live a little. I have an idea. Follow my lead."

Before Daniel could make a formal protest, he was watching Gretchen's hips swing from side to side. It was mesmerizing, especially in those stilettos. *How can she possibly walk that way and still stay upright? It's a true talent.*

Gretchen stopped mid-hallway and looked over her shoulder. "Are you coming?"

Daniel bounded out of the chair. "Of course. I was just admiring the view."

Gretchen took his arm. "As well you should. Now, let's go play. I believe the Malloy mojo magic is back."

"Is that a new thing?"

"Certainly not."

Daniel grabbed a shrimp appetizer as he passed a serving tray. "I've never heard about your magic before."

"Well, frankly, I never lost it, and we are going to use it to do good."

"Of course. We are the good guys. Do you want to enlighten me on your operation, Ms. Malloy?"

"No, it's better if you just play along. You are more comfortable that way."

Daniel's eyes lifted to the ceiling. "Oh Lord. I'm not going to like this, am I?"

"Perhaps not, but I promise to pay you back for your effort later tonight. Are you game?"

Daniel's sly smile gave her his answer. "I always enjoy how you pay me back. I'll play as long as I'm playing with you."

By the time they reached the couple, the man and woman seemed to be in a deep discussion.

"Diana, or should I say Andrea? What a surprise," Gretchen announced loudly. Daniel stood by as the event planner hugged the younger woman and nodded toward the tennis pro. "And Archer, it's been so long." She kissed the tennis pro on each cheek and added a full hug.

"Gretchen Malloy, how have you been?"

"I'm always marvelous. I'm not sure I'll ever play tennis again though after that tumble I took on the court several years ago. I just haven't had the hunger in my belly to be in traction for weeks after a serve. Do you two know each other?"

Daniel's head bowed down. *Take her lead, she said. She'd make it up to me. What in the hell is she doing?*

"Andrea is thinking about joining the club," Archer answered. Gretchen noticed the woman at his side gulp.

"Again?"

Gulping again, Andrea then took a large drink from her glass. The silence finally gave way to Andrea's uncomfortable answer. "I was never a real member."

"You were an associate. This little stinker changed her name to work for an attorney. Tricksters do get caught." Gretchen laughed as she shook her finger in the woman's direction. "I remember, but it was several years ago. Yes, it was the same year they found that body on the golf course. That year was unforgettable. I actually helped the membership committee vet prospects. I know you were sponsored by…what was his name?"

"Garrett."

Gretchen smiled. "Yes, Garrett, as in Mrs. Notte's grandson. Did you two know each other from social circles or were you dating? I can't recall."

Archer stepped forward and offered his hand to Daniel to squash the questioning. "I'm Archer Tate, the club's tennis pro, and you are?"

"Where are my manners?" Gretchen gushed like a geyser in a state park. "This is Daniel Williams. He's thinking about joining the club."

The two men shook hands, but Andrea added to the introduction. "He's a police detective investigating my former boss's murder."

"I am that, but I'm here for pleasure tonight, Diana, sorry Andrea." Daniel winked at Gretchen.

"Have they found the guy who did it?" the tennis pro asked. He seemed to be offering a buffer to Andrea.

"We have. In fact, we're thinking of closing the case within the week."

"Wonderful." Andrea's exclamation seemed to be a sense of relief.

That piqued Gretchen's attention. She melted onto Daniel's arm. "Yes, then we will have more time to be together. You see, we're making plans for our future."

Archer chuckled. "The great Gretchen Malloy is going to settle down, and with just one man?"

"Well, when you have the opportunity to have a man like this, you do. You see, Daniel can afford this club. He could actually buy it all on his own. Right, dear?"

"I don't like to talk about my money, darling. You know that." Daniel played the embarrassed rich man act to a tee.

"So, you're not really a detective?" Andrea was in a state of confusion.

"I am. I like to give back to the community, but I'm a trust fund heir, the only heir. I don't like to talk about how rich I am. It can make it so uncomfortable. You both understand, right?"

Both suspects nodded before Archer asked, "So what are your plans? Gretchen always has plans."

"Well, Daniel will join the club, and since it's near Mrs. Notte's lovely mansion, she's selling it to us. That's where we're making our home, well there and his family's private island. Oh, you should see it. It is paradise on earth."

"**You're** buying the Notte mansion?" Andrea's concern was in her voice.

"Yes. Mrs. Notte wanted to sell her home to someone she knew. Of course, Daniel could do it on his own, but I'm selling my place too. It's the least I can do. If I just contribute a bit–"

"Darling, we discussed this. You'll use your money for that special furniture in the refurbished living room."

"Refurbished?" This time Archer expressed his concern.

Daniel eyed them suspiciously. *This is fun, but it's gone on too long. Always know when to walk away.* "Actually, we are digging up the side and back gardens off of Mrs. Notte's sitting area. We want to put in a large entertainment center complete with a new pool, and inside billiards and poker tables, a custom bar…so many things."

"I'm surprised my boss didn't know about this," Andrea answered.

"Oh, dear, he didn't. With his passing, Mrs. Notte was so despondent that she just asked us if we would like the house, and we said yes! We are so excited. Dear Daniel, are we closing next week?"

"I believe we will on the fifteenth." Daniel acted as though he was searching across the room. He touched Gretchen's hand. "Marty is leaving. You wanted to say goodbye. We should see him off."

"Oh yes, of course. Take care Andrea. Archer, it was lovely seeing you again."

"Nice to meet you. I'll probably see you on the courts this summer."

Both suspects nodded and said their goodbyes. Gretchen looked back as they walked away to add, "Tootles."

"We needed to leave them hanging."

"I wondered what you were doing. Of course, you're right. It's like fishing. You set the bait, then wait, but don't wait too long. Marty isn't leaving." Gretchen whispered.

"No, but I needed to make up something to get us away. Your act could go on all night."

"Mister, you weren't too bad at your own performance."

"I never am bad at performing." Daniel winked.

"Well, there is that. Let's actually make your little lie the truth. I want to say goodbye to Marty, and then let's go home and see if you're up to whatever I throw at you in my meek attempt at making up. Then, even though it's a Sunday, I'm calling a realtor friend of mine. We need to set up an online presence of a sale on that house so Andrea will have an inclination of expediency. We'll definitely include Mrs. Notte in the ruse. She'll be thrilled to be in the conspiracy again."

"And so, the game of chicken begins," Daniel murmured.

Chapter Twenty-Two

"This will be fun!" Mrs. Notte clapped her hands, and Gretchen noticed a brightness to the elderly woman's face that hadn't been there since last year. She'd been an integral inclusion in a DEA operation in the capture of some very bad people that led to Lily nearly being killed by a hit woman.

"As far as everyone knows, even Barrett, Gretchen and I are purchasing your house for ten million," Daniel explained. "We're giving you cash, and then you're moving down to your island house until you decide where you want to live."

"Roger, Detective," the elderly woman answered gleefully. "This is wonderful."

"What is wonderful, Mrs. Notte?" one of the nurses asked as they entered the room.

"I'm selling my home to this lovely couple. We'll close on the fifteenth."

The nurse smiled but seemed a little upset by the news. "Do you think you should maybe contact someone to discuss the idea with family, a friend, or your attorney?"

"My family consists of a little girl and her family. My friends think it's a marvelous idea after what my winter has been like, and my attorney was murdered. I'm of sound mind. Besides, I have another home in Florida that will be perfect. Daniel, Gretchen, could you arrange for someone to pack up the home for me?"

"Of course. We can take care of everything," Gretchen said assuredly. She looked over at the nurse's name tag. "Jill, nothing nefarious is going on. This makes Mrs. Notte so happy, and we are thrilled to be able to do this."

"This will make the difference for me. I'll be closer to my great granddaughter, and the beach is always so therapeutic."

The nurse noticed the difference in her patient. "Wonderful. If everything is above board, then congratulations all around. Mrs. Notte, do you want your lunch in your room today?"

"No, I think I'll go to the dining room. I feel like a weight has been lifted off of me. I want to live again."

Daniel's brows furrowed. He grabbed Gretchen's hand as Mrs. Notte discussed her menu options. "Is she that good of an actress, or is she really selling us that mansion?"

"I'm not sure. Can we afford a house like that?"

Daniel thought for a second. "If that's what you want, then yes. It's a steal at ten million."

"You could live in one wing, and I'll live in the other. I could run my business from one of the first-floor rooms…the library would be perfect. If I lighten that wood up, add some color, have fresh flowers–"

"Stop." Daniel placed a finger up to Gretchen's red lipsticked lips. "Back to earth. We are setting up a sting, not your event parlor."

"Salon."

"Whatever," Daniel said calmly. "Mrs. Notte?"

"Oh yes, dear." The nurse smiled and left the room. "What is it, Detective?"

"You do realize we aren't really purchasing your home, right?"

"Of course. I was just acting. I love this cloak and dagger stuff, and obviously I'm very good at it. Did Carlos or Devlin recommend me for this operation, or do you prefer the term mission?"

Daniel smiled. "Actually, it's because you own the house everyone seems so interested in. So, one more time, do you have any idea if there's something in your home or on the property that may be hidden and may be of value to someone who knew your grandson?"

"Like the cartel?"

Daniel nodded. "Exactly. This has to be drug related considering the evidence and those who are involved."

"Well, I've been thinking since you asked me the last time you were here. Garrett and his father had so many secrets, but my husband was the same way. Garrett always used to tell his father they needed insurance. Of course, I thought they were speaking about insurance on art, the jewelry, the cars, or even on the house, but now—"

"I understand. It's exactly as I thought. Mrs. Notte, where would they have placed that insurance? Where would they hide things?"

"You know where the safe is. I alone used that. I didn't trust either one of them. I didn't always know what they were up to, but I knew they were up to no good of some kind. Again, I thought it had something to do with business, not drugs and larceny."

Gretchen began to say something, but Daniel waved her off. Mrs. Notte seemed to be weakening, or her memories of her family were sending her into a black hole.

They both stood and said their goodbyes. Once in the hallway, Gretchen seemed more determined than ever to end this crisis for the elderly woman. "She doesn't deserve this. She's never deserved her awful son or his evil spawn. She deserves peace."

Daniel placed his arm around her shoulders. "That's exactly why they used to call us peace officers."

"Funny man." Gretchen nudged his rib cage but gave him a peck on the cheek. "Thank you for doing this. I know you don't have to, but you are such a sweet man."

"Stop saying that. I'm not that sweet. I want to get these people. Who knows? Our bait may catch a big fish or two."

"I do like to go fishing!"

Chapter Twenty-Three

The bait was set; the ruse was continuing. Gretchen called in a favor and had a designer come to the house to begin the redecorating and renovation plans.

Two weeks later, Mrs. Notte was released from the rehab center and returned to her home…for now. She enjoyed the play they were performing. The next day would be the fifteenth, and hopefully Andrea and whoever would play their hand in this dangerous game.

Barrett opened the large door to Gretchen. "I brought her favorite cookies, and for you I found your pistachio almond ice cream."

The tall man leaned down and hugged her. "Thank you for all you do."

"It's nothing, really. How is she today?"

Gretchen made her way in and noticed Mrs. Notte was sitting in the sunspot of her favorite room.

"She is content, Ms. Malloy. Lily called last night around dinner time. We were able to connect the video so Mrs. Notte could see the children. Andrew seems to be growing quickly."

"Little Drew will be tall like his dad. I'm thinking of putting Emi in ballet. What do you think?"

"Excellent idea for a young lady, but perhaps you should check with her parents before paying for said class?"

"Pish, posh, Barrett. You know they'd say to wait, but I believe it's never too early to establish the ground rules for grace and balance. That's how I've lasted this long in my heels."

As Gretchen sashayed by the loyal employee, he murmured he'd always wondered about how she did it.

"Look what I brought for my favorite woman in all of Kansas City." Gretchen held the box up high as though it was a trophy.

Mrs. Notte smiled widely. "My cookies?"

"Of course. Napkins are in the box. Barrett, do you think we could have coffee?"

"Of course. Coming right up." He left quickly to stow his ice cream as well.

While the two ladies oohed and ahhed over the beautifully decorated butter cookies from one of the oldest bakeries in the city, Gretchen thought she heard a crash in the kitchen. With such a big house, the sound reverberated. *It's probably just the trash pickup down the street.*

"No police or security today?" Gretchen wondered.

"Oh no, dear. They aren't here during the day. I suppose they figure the bad guys wouldn't be that brazen to attack while the sun is up, but I feel very secure at night. Did you know your detective stayed the night on Tuesday?"

"I do. Isn't he just the sweetest?"

"I suppose. He's very brave, and although I'm old, I've noticed he is very handsome. He loves you, you know."

Gretchen glowed. "Oh, I know. I love him too. I say that proudly."

"Good. Don't allow that one to get away. Where is Barrett?"

Gretchen stood up. "He had to make a pot. I can check on him." She glanced down at the back hallway but saw no movement. She heard a shuffling noise. Something was wrong. She texted Daniel quickly and just hit three numbers...9-1-1. "Mrs. Notte, I need you to remain calm, and play your part. I think we have intruders."

Mrs. Notte turned and grabbed the nearby fireplace poker. "I do not have guns in the home so arm yourself. There's an autographed baseball over there in the corner. Grab it."

Before Gretchen's heels could carry her to the other side of the room, three figures entered the sitting room. This was it. Andrea didn't even bother to disguise herself, neither did the two rather large men on either side of her.

"Now that we have both of you here at the same time, and we will not have any interruptions of any kind, we need to end this. Ms. Malloy, sit down on the couch. Mrs. Notte, drop that poker. Now."

"Young lady, you are a disappointment," Mrs. Notte reprimanded. She dropped her instrument of menace, and it was immediately grabbed by one of the men. He also collected Gretchen's cell phone.

"My phone is my entire life, my business. Give that back."

Andrea grinned. "Then maybe your life will be over today. You won't need it, Ms. Malloy. Ladies, we have a little problem."

"What do you want?" Mrs. Notte demanded.

"Your grandson hid a very important item from me. I want it back today. I'm done trying to figure it out. But old lady, or you, the most irritating woman I've met knows where it is."

"Is it Garrett's insurance just in case you turned on him? Apparently, you finally have. I suppose honor among thieves is over." Gretchen's tone remained cool and in control, but her heart was frantic. She hadn't heard a return from Daniel. There was no text, no call. *Daniel, where are you when we really need you?*

Chapter Twenty-Four

"Dev, I'm doing seventy on Broadway."

"Did she say what was going on?"

"No. I've sent a patrol over there, but no lights or sirens."

Devlin Pierce paced in his office as he listened to the usually cool and calm Daniel Williams. Gretchen and Mrs. Notte were in danger. Even though he was on the other side of the nation, he felt the same fear. He didn't dare mention any of this to Lily until everything went down, and safely.

"Daniel, this is what I found out. I remembered who Ross really is. He was the brother-in-law of my American contact for the Sinaloa cartel. I arranged meetings with him a couple of times over the telephone while I was in Miami. Once I put all of that together, you have to know that Andrea could be more dangerous. She's a killer."

"What? Are you kidding me?"

"I wish I were. They are all related either by blood or cartel. One of our agents spoke to Garrett. Andrea is the one who involved him in the drug world. There's some tennis pro—"

"I met him before Mrs. Notte was released back to the house. I figured he was the contact in the club. That was his main market. Get the hell out of the way."

Daniel hit a traffic jam as he approached The Plaza. "Dev, how do I play this?"

"They're looking for Garrett's insurance. It was a book he lifted off of Andrea years ago, and it has all of her contacts from the top to the bottom. He says there was even a cop's name in there and a minister who got caught up with his own drug abuse. But the focus of that book was the names of all the big players, the contacts, locations of drops, everything. She wants that book."

"But no one knows where it is." Daniel Williams wound his way onto Ward Parkway and met up with three patrol cars who had blocked off the street two blocks down from Mrs. Notte's home. Neighbors were coming out to watch the action. They were quickly greeted by police with guns drawn and commands to stay in their homes.

"My agent bartered some privileges for Garrett and discovered that when they were on better terms, he told Andrea he buried it with his puppy."

"He had a puppy? Great. Where the hell would he put the dog?"

"The book is buried under a bench in Mrs. Notte's garden. He put it there because that's where his grandparents always sat to watch the sunset. Maybe he does have a heart?"

"Then why were they looking inside the house?"

"That's another story. We'll talk later, but there's stolen art under some of those paintings thanks to Bernard

Notte. The FBI will send a unit once this is all finished, but I had a team who left early this morning. Their ETA should be right about now." Dev looked down at his phone and saw the text. "Daniel, they're down the street from you. The lead agent is Perry Foster. He's a good guy. They know you're the one calling the shots."

Daniel held his gun in one hand and his cell in the other as he ran down the back of the property. One patrol car sat in the same location Lily and Gretchen had performed the great stakeout. "Thanks. Dev, I'm here. I'm getting that damn book. I'll update later."

"Good luck, Daniel."

An officer ran up to him, "Detective Williams, we have a good view right through this gap in the fence."

The DEA agent stood waiting for the detective. "I'm Foster. You must be Williams."

"Yes, thanks for coming."

"We ran into a little issue at the airport, or we would've been here sooner. I'll fill you in later." The DEA agent handed him a vest and he quickly put it on.

Daniel nodded and directed his attention once more to the tactical police officer. "Fine. Officer, get the bolt cutters and open that gate over there. I'm going into that garden, and I need a shovel too."

Chapter Twenty-Five

All Gretchen could do was stall the invaders. *The plan worked. The fish are just a little too big for me to reel in.* "Andrea, what does this insurance look like? Has anyone but you seen it, or is it a figment of your very active imagination? We know you like to play act, have a different persona—"

"You have a big mouth, lady. Just shut up and sit there." She looked down at Gretchen's heels. "Remove those."

"What?"

"You heard me. Take those heels off. I don't need you using those things as weapons."

Gretchen folded her arms defiantly and straightened her back. "I will not be without my heels."

Andrea wielded her gun in her direction. "Tomas, take them off of her. From what I've heard, she's wily, and I don't need some meddling wedding planner messing this up."

In one move, Andrea's soldier jerked off Gretchen's very expensive, red-bottomed shoes. "Ow, you animal! By the way, I'm not just a wedding planner. I am an elite event planner. I don't meddle; I involve myself."

"Shut up. You don't have your idiot detective, your fawning senator, and that butler guy is out cold in the kitchen. Now, ladies, I want what I want." One of her accomplices stood next to her, leaning on a shovel.

"But what do you want? I don't know what you want, do you Mrs. Notte?"

"Shut up, Ms. Malloy."

"Andrea, you need to be more specific. Mrs. Notte is quite old, and her memory is waning. I, on the other hand, have a selective memory, and I really don't feel like helping you."

"That's fine. You'll be useful anyway." Andrea walked behind the seated Gretchen and placed her gun against the back of her head. "Mrs. Notte, you will tell me where it is, or I'll make sure Ms. Malloy never irritates anyone again."

Mrs. Notte nervously hit the arms of her chair with her hands. "What do you want? My grandson never told me what he was doing. I didn't know. I didn't know about either of them and their criminal activity," Mrs. Notte screamed out.

"You really don't know. What the hell?" Andrea began to pace. "Fine, he hid it where he buried the blasted dog, the puppy."

Mrs. Notte glanced at Gretchen. Gretchen bit her lip. *Oh no! There was never a puppy! Damn Garrett Notte.* "My curiosity is getting the best of me. Since you'll probably kill us both when you get it, what exactly did he bury, and why were you searching in the house?"

"Why should I tell you?"

"Humor us. Maybe it will help Mrs. Notte remember," Gretchen said calmly.

"Fine, it's a damn ledger, a book. He stole it from me. I thought it was in the house, but my contact in Garrett's prison claims he was squealing to the feds and told them the truth about its location. He sold his information for ice cream, or lack of laundry duties."

"There really is no honor among thieves. What is the world coming to?"

"Your world is ending, Ms. Malloy. I may let the old lady live so she can watch you die. I'm just tired of you. Now, Mrs. Notte, I hope my story telling has jogged your memory. Where did he bury that damn dog?"

"In the garden?" Mrs. Notte's voice shook with emotion.

"Well, no kidding. Where in the garden?"

"Let me think." Now, Mrs. Notte was stalling. "Garrett was twelve when the dog died. The puppy acquired a very rare disease. What was that disease? It was some form of blood cancer. The vet had never seen a case of it in such a young dog. Garrett was so upset. We offered to get him another one, but he wanted–"

"Stop. Where is the dog buried?"

"We had the puppy cremated."

Gretchen's snickering only got her a blank stare from the two men, and a glare from Andrea. *Daniel will get here. I trust him. I have faith in him. I don't want to die.*

"Mrs. Notte, my patience is over. Exactly where is the damn dog buried? Tell me, we'll get the book, and be gone."

"And you'll let us all live?" Now the elderly woman was bargaining.

"Just tell me. You're out of time." Andrea turned and shot at a photo of Mrs. Notte and her late husband. "The next bullet goes into Ms. Malloy's head."

"Stop talking about shooting Ms. Malloy. Fine, the puppy was buried next to the gate at the back of the property. There's a blue spruce there at the gap in the fence. When Garrett was young, he used to sneak back into the house through that space. He buried the puppy there." Mrs. Notte held her head in her hands and began to cry.

Gretchen wanted to applaud the performance, but the entire situation wasn't entertaining. This was dire.

"Manno, go get it." The man in jeans and a black shirt, headed through the patio double doors out into the garden with his shovel. "Now, we wait." Andrea took a position near the patio doors. She leaned against the bookcases.

All three women were silent. Andrea's attention roamed from her hostages to what little she could see of the garden. Spring flowers, trees, and bushes were beginning to bloom yielding very few views from the sitting room except for a maze of color.

Andrea looked up at the clock. "What is taking so long? Tomas, go out there and help Manno. We need to dig it up and get out of here. Ms. Malloy may have a tracker on her, and we don't need the police."

Did Daniel put a tracker on me? I hope he did. That would be an invasion of my privacy, but I don't care at this moment. Gretchen giggled unnaturally. "Funny you should say that."

"Why's that?" Andrea's other cohort exited through the doors.

"You see we've been playing you. I do have a tracker on me, and a recorder. The police are hearing everything you're saying, and they know what you're doing."

Andrea smiled. "I know that's not true, Ms. Malloy. Our organization is very wealthy, and I began jamming any GPS signals when we arrived. As for your recording device, I sincerely doubt you have one, but I've jammed anything like that as well. If it's in this house, it's disabled."

Gretchen arched her left brow. "Really? Are you sure? You seem like a very bright young lady, but I'm a pro at this sort of thing. I've taken down better than you."

Andrea shifted her attention back to the garden. The two female captives exchanged glances. Gretchen noticed a reflection. The light had somehow shifted the stream through the patio doors. The bright light blinded her. *What in the world is shining in?* She barely saw a gun pointed around the edge of the side of the home. *The cavalry's here!*

She needed to distract the woman with the gun. Gretchen motioned with her eyes toward Mrs. Notte. She was attempting to have the elderly woman send something in the room flying, crashing, falling over, whatever would work as a distraction. Mrs. Notte finally understood. She reached into the side of her chair and pulled out long knitting needles and yarn.

"I think I'll make your nice detective a sweater. It'll take me at least until the end of summer to complete it."

Andrea jumped toward the matron. "Where did you get those?" She grabbed both needles and yards of yarn followed. "You're a crazy lady."

By the time Andrea set the items on the bookcase near Gretchen's stilettos, two forms, and not Andrea's accomplices, were closer to the doors. Sadly, they opened the patio doors at the same time the woman turned. Her gun was pointed directly at them, theirs were on her.

"Drop it, Andrea," Daniel ordered. "Now."

"You have no way out," the other man informed her. "We have the house surrounded by KCPD and DEA agents. You're done."

Andrea grinned and turned the gun on Mrs. Notte. "Not yet. I have a move. I'll shoot the old lady. Mrs. Notte come over here."

"What should I do?" The helpless woman looked toward Gretchen for an answer. Daniel nodded.

"Go ahead, if you can. Wait, Andrea, use me. Mrs. Notte can barely walk. We can get out faster, and you can even take my car."

"Oh no. You probably do have a tracker on that. I don't think the detective trusts you, Ms. Malloy." She briefly thought then trained her gun on Gretchen. "Okay, yes, you get up and join me. We're going to be leaving together."

"Andrea," Daniel called out calmly. "You won't even make it across the state line, and you and I both know the nearest interstate is miles away. The traffic will be awful at this time of the day. What's your move? Where do you think you're going?"

"To the downtown airport. I'll be flying out. Your whatever she is will be joining me until the plane is almost ready to take off. I'll dump her out. She has enough meat on her bones. She probably won't break anything. Move, Ms. Malloy, now."

Gretchen stood up slowly. "Daniel, it will be fine." Mrs. Notte began to wail, but Andrea ignored the drama. "What about my shoes?"

Andrea touched the stilettos briefly as if she was almost going to allow the woman her footwear. "No. Barefoot is better. You'll be slower. I've seen you walk in those things."

As they began to back out of the room, Andrea called someone and spoke in Spanish. When she ended the discussion, she was almost out in the hallway. "Detective, don't get any wild ideas about sending all the police downtown. I have twenty men on that plane. We are all heavily armed. If you get out of line while Ms. Malloy and I are having our pleasant trip to the airport, I'll kill her. You'll find her with a bullet in her head. Understand?"

Daniel's usually soft gray eyes were almost the color of steel. He caught Gretchen's gaze. He offered a supportive smile. "I understand. G, I'm sorry you won't have your shoes. Take care of those beautiful feet."

"I do feel naked without my stilettos. You know, they're not only a fashion statement, they're a financial investment." Gretchen made a sniffing noise as if she was going to burst into tears.

"Oh, for the sake of God, they're just shoes you ignorant woman!" Andrea lowered the gun briefly as she complained.

Gretchen reached out to her left and picked up one of the stilettos. She drove the six-inch heel into the side of Andrea's leg. Quickly she picked up the other one and stuck it into her arm. With the movement, Daniel was able to run toward the two and grab the gun. Agent Foster continued to direct his gun on the writhing young woman.

Gretchen stood up, brushed her hair with her hands, and went to Mrs. Notte's side. "And they aren't just shoes!" She yelled in defiance. "They can be weapons, distractions, hammers, but I don't really recommend it. I've also used them as a screwdriver in a pinch, oh, and I tapped a welcome sign up at a wedding venue once with my blue ones."

"Are those the ones with the butterfly brooches?" Mrs. Notte asked.

"Yes, that's right."

"I've always loved those, dear." Mrs. Notte reached up and held Gretchen's hand while the multitude of police and agents flowed into the home from every direction.

Daniel and Foster were too busy handcuffing the cartel family member. "Oh, and all of your men have already been carted away, Andrea. We flew in on the opposite end of the airport. We were a little late to the party here because of the welcoming party we had down there. You can hear about it on the news tonight."

As she was removed from the room, Andrea snarled back at Gretchen. Daniel heaved a very large sigh as he finally holstered his gun. He shook his head as he walked over to Gretchen and Mrs. Notte. "Mrs. Notte, you were marvelous. That was very brave of you."

"Oh Daniel, you have no idea. She was brilliant. You really should've been an actress." Gretchen's highly animated compliments made the elderly woman blush.

"No, my dear, you were the star. Detective, you truly have someone special here."

Daniel broke his own rules and took Gretchen into his arms. "Oh, she's special alright. We call her the stiletto terrorist, and now Andrea will tell the tale of how she was taken down by a pair of heels."

"I always told you my shoes were very important, and now you know."

"I know a lot of things. I know I was scared to death that I would lose you, and I know I can't live without you."

Gretchen playfully touched his tie. "And I'm the most intriguing, captivating, enchanting woman you've ever–"

"Irritating, impulsive, invasive…that sounds like I'm describing poison ivy," Daniel said with a straight face.

Gretchen kissed his cheek. "I don't give you a rash."

Daniel bobbed his head back and forth in thought. "So far." He kissed her back. "I'm not sure I'll ever get used to how you think, and I'm okay with that. It makes life very interesting."

Barrett walked slowly into the room. Mrs. Notte was surprised at how her loyal helper looked. "Oh, my goodness. He needs help."

A policewoman was helping him to the sofa. "We have paramedics arriving in a minute. I'd say he's going to have a very bad headache."

"They hit me over the head with a frying pan," he admitted.

Gretchen told Daniel to do what he needed to do while she stayed with Mrs. Notte and helped the devoted butler. She insisted the poor man have a glass of water, and she brought in a wet towel to begin to wipe the blood from his forehead and scalp. The paramedics quickly moved in and began their examination. They agreed he needed to go to the hospital, but he wanted to stay with his employer.

"I'll stay with her until you come back, and if you have to stay overnight there, then I'll stay the night. Don't you worry," Gretchen assured him.

Within a couple of hours most of the law enforcers had departed Mrs. Notte's home. The FBI would arrive early in the morning to look over every piece of artwork in the house. After Gretchen made sandwiches for Mrs. Notte and herself, she had the elderly woman take her medication. She even managed to get the woman upstairs for a late afternoon nap. Even Gretchen put her feet up and closed her eyes on a lovely chaise lounge in the hallway near the master bedroom.

It was nearly five o'clock when Gretchen and Mrs. Notte began to decide what dinner would look like. The doorbell made them both jump.

Gretchen looked out and saw a familiar handsome face. "Daniel! And you have food!"

"I thought you two might need something, and I brought one more thing…"

Barrett stood behind him. With a large bandaid over his eyes and a bandage on his head, the man looked a little worse for wear. "I just have to be careful."

"Get in here, both of you. Barrett, she's been so worried about you."

Daniel managed a quick kiss with his woman as the butler walked slowly toward Mrs. Notte. The elderly woman began to cry. As he crouched down to hold her hand, Mrs. Notte touched his face softly. "My faithful Winslow. You missed all of the action."

"I hope you and Ms. Malloy will regale me with stories during dinner. Detective Williams brought your favorite barbecue, Madame."

"That's very kind, but all I really want is to make sure you're absolutely okay."

He nodded. "I just need to take it easy."

Daniel held up the bags of food. "Mrs. Notte, where do you eat this kind of food? I doubt you watch television and eat ribs."

"Oh, you have no idea. Detective, there's a hidden television in that corner cabinet, and there's trays in the closet. We will eat here. Thank you for providing our meal. This is so very kind of you."

Gretchen snuggled against his arm. "That's what you are, Daniel. You are the kindest man I have ever known. Well, there is Devlin, but Mr. Delicious isn't here."

Daniel set the bags on a side table. "When do I receive my moniker? And what will it be? I like Mr. Delicious, but since that's already in use–"

Gretchen opened the cabinet in the corner, and helped Barrett to sit on one of the large chairs that also had an ottoman for his legs. "You don't need a nickname, Daniel."

Daniel retrieved the trays and began to set them up in front of Mrs. Notte and the butler. Once he neared the elaborate coffee table in front of the sofa, he grimaced. Placemats flew in front of his face.

"Barbecue can be messy." Gretchen stood proudly, holding two more mats and several napkins she'd found in the television cabinet.

Daniel began to place the plastic containers out on the large table. "I still want a nickname. It's not fair that Dev has one, and I don't."

"We will talk about it later tonight."

"Why can't we talk about it now?"

Gretchen stamped one foot. "We will talk about it privately, later tonight. Do you understand?"

Daniel looked up from the open coleslaw and grinned. "Oh. Privately."

Gretchen licked her lips. "Yes, very privately."

Chapter Twenty-Six

"It's very nice down here."

"Yes, very nice." Months later, Gretchen and Daniel sat on the beach in front of Mrs. Notte's large home near Bean Point. "I don't believe I've ever been on Anna Maria Island before."

"It's pretty. That house is amazing, and this view is unbelievable. I like the fact that everyone uses the nightly sunset as their entertainment," Daniel commented. He looked over at their elderly host and Barrett. They were sipping iced tea. As soon as the sun fell into the water, they would all go in for dinner and drinks.

"Has Dev and the DEA finished with that blasted ledger?"

"Heaven's no. There's enough intel in that thing to keep them busy for years. Of course, some of it is old and useless, but it does seem to show the pattern of the cartel's shipping and business, including very valuable dealers and their locations. Oh, and the country club needs a new tennis pro."

"So sad." Gretchen clutched her neck as though she actually was in pain over the news. "He was obnoxious. What about the artwork? Mrs. Notte said the FBI is examining each and every piece of art and jewelry in her house."

Daniel chuckled. "And she's loving every minute of it. They're finished. They've tested and photographed. Some pieces will need to have an additional analysis. Andrea and her gang are jailed. That insurance company is being investigated, and all of Gilliard's accounts, jewelry, furnishings, and everything from the kitchen sink is being examined. The wife is beside herself. You and I don't own a home."

"Yet." Gretchen kissed her detective on the cheek.

Daniel returned her kiss. "Mrs. Notte said she'd actually sell it to us. You could have your business there. It would be sweet."

"No. I like my apartment. I'll continue to meet my clients at their place, at their event venues, or at their church.""It is a nice place with a great view of The Plaza, especially when the holiday lights come on Thanksgiving night." Daniel looked down at his watch. "Anytime now."

"I can't wait," Gretchen admitted. "I'm not very good with secrets."

"I wouldn't say that." Daniel nuzzled her neck and kissed the top of her bare shoulder.

"I hear them." Gretchen looked past Daniel to see a young girl leading a toddler. Behind the running children, the adults followed. Gretchen could clearly make out Lily and Alise. Both babies were being carried by their fathers.

"Nanny."

"Notey."

Gretchen turned to watch Mrs. Notte's reaction. Barrett pointed his finger in the direction of the beach.

The woman began to cry, her hand held up to her mouth in surprise.

Angelica ran ahead to hug her great grandmother. Andrew bounded by Gretchen and Daniel and hugged her as well. "Nanny, we're surprising you," Angelica said with a large smile.

"Notey." Andrew patted Mrs. Notte's arm.

"What is he saying?" Mrs. Notte patted his head.

"I think he's trying to say your name, so he put Nanny and your name together. Mommy and Daddy are here too, see?"

"Oh my goodness. Everyone is here. Barrett, do we have enough food?"

"Yes, Madame. I knew about the surprise. There's a chef preparing a magnificent meal in the kitchen right now."

"Oh good. I wouldn't want to be a poor hostess."

"Well, that could never happen," Lily commented as she walked past Gretchen and Daniel.

Mrs. Notte reached out for the adults. "Lily, Devlin, Alise, and Carlos, I'm beside myself with happiness. I'm overwhelmed."

Lily kissed the elderly woman on the cheek. "There's nowhere we would rather be than with you."

Mrs. Notte leaned into Lily and whispered. "Is there another operation your dear husband needs me for? You can ask the detective. I'm rather good at playing my part."

"Oh, we know. We are all just here for you and to enjoy being together."

Mrs. Notte nodded. These people were her family. "Barrett, I need to get inside to see if that chef is up to par."

"Yes, Madame, but I believe he is one of the best in the entire Tampa Bay area."

Mrs. Notte waved her hand at her butler. "Barrett."

"Yes, Mrs. Notte." He shrugged and turned to the others. "We will see you all inside." He looked at his wristwatch. "Twenty minutes should suffice."

"Barrett," Mrs. Notte said.

"Yes, Madame, into the house we go." He began pushing his dear employer's wheelchair up to the house.

"I think we better go with them," Alise announced. She picked Emi out of Dev's arms. "We'll take the children."

"I think I want a ride like Mrs. Notte's." Carlos watched as Barrett entered the house with his companion. "Those beach wheelchairs are cool."

"Come on, you. Maybe she'll let you take a spin tomorrow." Alise pulled on her husband's shirt leaving the two couples alone on the beach.

Minutes later, Lily ditched her sandals to begin the walk up to the house. "There's nothing better than toes in the sand."

Gretchen huffed. "I wouldn't say that. A pair of leather Italian heels from Florence is far superior."

"But you can't wear stilettos in the sand."

"Really?" Gretchen's arched brow told her friend she meant business. "Just watch me." Gretchen rose from her seat in the sand, placed her heels on her feet, and began to walk slowly.

"No fair, you're walking on the hard part," Lily yelled. "Try walking where it's soft."

"No problem, Lily. You just divert your weight to the front. Just like life, you hold your head up and keep pushing forward. Like this." Gretchen's hips swayed as she walked slowly up to the house.

"How does she do that?" Lily watched in awe. For years she had noticed Gretchen and those long legs, feet housed in stilettos that could rush around a reception venue changing out incorrect place cards.

Daniel adored that woman. "She does it in great style and with those beautiful legs. She has such a zest for life, doesn't she?"

Lily nodded. Gretchen did hold onto life as though it was a life preserver in a stormy ocean. "Ah, you're a leg man. No wonder you like Gretchen."

"Nope, I'm a Gretchen lover, the whole insane package."

Dev walked on the other side of Daniel. He placed a friendly arm over his shoulders. "Daniel, we need to talk about some things. Have you visited a doctor recently, preferably a psychiatrist?"

"You know, I probably should, Dev. She makes me angry, sad, happy, and infuriated all on the same day, but there's just something about her."

Dev shook his head in defeat. "You've got it bad."

"No, Dev. I've got it good. I've got Gretchen Malloy. I'm going to run up ahead. I need to ask her something, and this is the perfect time to do it."

Lily stopped in her tracks. "He isn't, is he? He would do it in front of us. We are her friends. Oh my gosh, look he just got down on one knee."

"Lily, it could be something completely different than what you're thinking. But he is on one knee, and he just pulled something out of his pocket."

"What's he saying? Can you hear?"

"No, but we can move a little closer."

Nearer the house, Gretchen looked down at Daniel. "Did you drop something?"

"Yes, and I need to shake the sand out of this shoe. Here, take a look at this photo." Daniel handed it up to Gretchen.

"I know him. I'm planning his daughter's very elaborate wedding for Labor Day weekend."

Daniel's arm reached around Gretchen's back. "Well, I've been meaning to ask you about a wedding. Of course, it involves you."

Gretchen wondered. *What is he asking? Obviously, it has something to do with the wedding I'm planning, or...* "Daniel, what is it? What do you want to ask me?"

"I know you have your professional principles, but we have a case involving your client, and I was wondering–"

"Are you asking me, dear man what I think you're asking me?"

Daniel stood up. His voice was a little shaky. "I think so?"

"Oh Daniel! Of course I will." Gretchen hugged him tightly. She noticed Lily jumping up and down in some sort of celebration. "What is wrong with her?"

"Who her?"

"Lily." Gretchen pulled away. "Lily, what is your problem?"

"I'm so happy for you and Daniel. Congratulations." Lily hugged both of them as Dev delayed his reaction. In his line of business, misinterpreting body language could get you killed.

"Daniel, I think Lily thought something else was going on. She thought we had something to celebrate." Dev moved to stand next to him.

Gretchen searched Lily's joy filled face. "Oh, Lily! Daniel just asked me to be his inside man. That didn't sound right. He asked me to be his undercover woman. Well, now that's just lovely and delicious sounding, isn't it?" Gretchen threw back her hair and laughed. "Daniel, that is what you were asking isn't it?"

Daniel was totally confused at the scene playing out in front of him. "Lily, we have an ongoing investigation of one of Gretchen's clients. I'm wanting her to keep her ears open and pick up any intel she can. She's proved over and over that she is a very effective amateur sleuth."

"Isn't that the sweetest thing you've ever heard?" Gretchen was giddy, delighted that she would be included on a real investigation with no threat of arrest or imprisonment. She grabbed Dev's hand and pulled him along. "Come on, Mr. Delicious. We do have so many things to celebrate."

Lily remained behind with Daniel. They looked at each other. "I thought–"

Daniel's hands went into his pockets. "I know what you thought. That was funny…the kneeling, handing her something, and her sheer delight at the very thought she could go undercover."

"It's none of my business, but I have to ask. Marriage? Is it even remotely an idea for the two of you?"

"Lily, we've got a good thing going. I'm moving in with her by August. She's happy. I'm happy, in fact I'm the happiest I've been in years. She is the reason as crazy as that may sound."

"So, no more headaches?"

Daniel opened the door to the house. "I'll be honest. With Gretchen Malloy, I'm afraid those headaches will return occasionally."

Lily pointed a finger in his direction. "Don't forget the tapping, the clicking, all that red, the drama–"

"And those damn stilettos?"

Lily shared a laugh with him before they reached the others who were already sitting at the dining table. "You will have to pry those off of her cold, dead feet before she'll lose those."

Daniel leaned down to whisper. "Oh, naive woman. I have my ways to get those heels off quickly. I can be very effective when necessary, and I'm the one who legally has the handcuffs."

Lily snorted. "But yours aren't soft and fuzzy like hers."

Daniel agreed. "And animal print! Then there's the ones in her signature hot red color, the pink ones with the hearts–"

Lily leaned on one of the formal chairs before sitting as she laughed hard and loud.

"What are you two hysterical about?" Gretchen asked. Lily's face was beginning to turn red as a beet.

Lily couldn't speak. She tried, but nothing came out of her mouth. Daniel cleared his throat to finally answer.

"We were talking about necessary accessories for the woman who seems to have everything," Daniel answered as he took his seat next to the object of the discussion.

"You will tell me later," Gretchen whispered.

"Oh, darling, I'll even show you." Daniel added a wink.

"Daniel? You're beginning to sound like me. How splendid!" *What has happened to my sweet man? Oh well, more fun for me.*

Chapter Twenty-Seven

The wedding of the year on Labor Day weekend was about to begin, but Gretchen wasn't as happy with her planning as she usually was. "Daniel, I believe I have a situation." Gretchen had to whisper. She couldn't take the chance that her client, his daughter, or anyone else at the hotel found her.

"Where are you? I'm heading your way right now." Daniel grabbed his jacket, motioned for his partner Jerry, and continued walking out of the police department offices.

"I'm in a maintenance closet near the elevator on the ballroom level. The staff hid me in here."

"Why?"

"It is imperative that **he** doesn't find me."

Damn, I put her in this position. Gretchen already had this man and his daughter as her clients. This was supposed to be an easy way for us to get information on him. I thought Gretchen would be safe.

"Has he attacked you? Is there a gun involved?"

His partner looked surprised at the questions. He wondered if they could get to Gretchen in time.

"Oh no, not yet. Daniel, he keeps pinching my butt."

Jerry continued to drive like a bat out of hell. They were only blocks away from the newest hotel in Kansas City. The client rented two entire floors for the wedding reception and guests' accommodations. Daniel thought Gretchen might hear something that could give a lead on her client's illegal activity. Undercover FBI agents were already in place acting as hotel support staff. They were even providing staging in the reception venue, complete with the latest devices for listening and photographing.

"What? He's pinching your butt? That's it? He didn't threaten you? "

Gretchen scoffed at the questions. "I think it's outrageous. He made suggestions."

"Such as?" Daniel crossed his eyes as he glanced at Jerry.

"He said he would pay to sleep with me. He said I was one hot mama. He should be shot for using that kind of language. The man has no manners or grace. Who raised him? Who says things like that? Besides, he could never afford me."

"Um, darling, he is suspected of white-collar crimes such as wire transfer fraud, among other things. He's not known to be an animal or dangerous."

"Well, he needs to be taught a lesson. I hope you all get the goods on him tonight during the reception. I'm not sure how long I can stall him."

"We're almost there. We'll come in without our badges so don't blow our cover, okay?"

"Me? I'm a professional investigator. I know how to act, remember?"

"We're here. Hang in there. We'll see you in just a few minutes."

"Please hurry, Daniel. I think I hear him coming. It is him. Lord, now he's suggesting we go to the nearest restroom. Who does he think I am? I would never do it in a restroom, well there was that time in Pittsburgh, but I'd say that was more of a fling. Oh, I have forgotten about the time at the aquarium."

"Stop G."

"Yes, Daniel. I'll be waiting. Please hurry."

The call ended as Daniel got out of the car. He had heard a man's voice yelling Gretchen's name. "Jerry, he wants to pay her to sleep with him."

"The man has no idea. I'd feel sorry for him." Jerry smiled at his friend as they entered the hotel. "The stairs are over here."

"Hey, she's mine."

Jerry nodded. "I know, and I worry about you. At the picnic last month, we all decided we would pray for you, but on the other hand my wife enjoyed Gretchen's company. She said your lady is going to offer free classes for the wives and girlfriends on planning an event on a budget. They're thrilled. Gretchen is nice. She's just too, too—"

"The word is *much*, Jerry." The two detectives rushed toward the elevators, searching for what might look like a maintenance closet. Instead of discovering a closet, they heard a scuffle of some kind down a hallway near the restrooms.

As they rounded the corner, they both stopped.

"Ow. Ow. You're hurting me with that. I promise to be good. Stop it. Ooh, that felt good."

"No, it isn't supposed to feel good, you animal. I will continue to work this evening, but you will stay away from me. Any payment you make to me will be for my services at your daughter's wedding. A gratuity will be required given the situation you and I find ourselves in. Do you understand?"

"Yes, yes, please just remove the broom and stop grounding your heel into my back."

"I'm going to remove the broomstick from your backside, and now I'm lifting my heel off of your back. Get up and be with your daughter."

"Yes, Ms. Malloy."

Daniel and Jerry held their hands up to their mouths to mask the amusement they were finding in the scene before them. "Well, she did seem to have it in hand," Jerry whispered.

The slightly embarrassed father of the bride passed them with his head lowered. He hurriedly zipped his fly and attempted to straighten his bow tie and tuxedo jacket.

Daniel looked down the hall to see Gretchen standing proudly with a broom in one hand as though it was her musket at Concord. She wore a classic pants suit, a tunic jacket with slim pants all in golden raw silk. Naturally, she wore red stilettos and every piece of red jewelry, diamonds and rubies, that Daniel had gifted her. "Um, are you okay, darling?"

"Oh Daniel, I am now. It was awful. The man is almost seventy. I don't want to see anything like that ever again. Please don't get old."

Jerry couldn't contain himself. "I'm going to meet you at the car. I'm happy to see you're okay, Gretchen."

"Thank you, Jerry. I appreciate the concern, but it seems I can handle it all on my own."

Daniel stopped his partner. "You know, I think I'll finish the twenty minutes left of my shift here. Are you okay with that?"

"Sure. Enjoy your day off tomorrow. Goodnight and good luck." Jerry began to walk away, then took two steps back to lean into Daniel. "I think you need an intervention of some kind. I just haven't figured it all out in my head yet."

"Will it make you feel better, if I agree with you, including the part about not figuring it out?"

"That's the first step to healing, to understand you do have a problem, albeit a tall, over-the-top, woman who never met a pair of heels she didn't love."

Daniel tapped his friend and partner on the shoulder. "Thanks, Jerry. See you Monday." *Now, what to do with Gretchen.*

Gretchen threw down the broom and rushed into Daniel's arms. He enveloped her quickly with a strong, secure embrace. "Oh, it was awful. He walked toward me and began to undress. Unless a man has a body, well, like you, I don't want to see any part, muscle, pimple, nothing. He said he knew I wanted him. How absolutely ridiculous! I mean, really!"

"Ridiculous indeed. Besides, you're all mine." He soothed her by smoothing her hair and rubbing her back. "Should I get you a drink?"

Gretchen pulled back. "Oh no, dear man. I have work to do." She looked him up and down. "Well, you'll have to do, even though you should be in a black tuxedo." She straightened his tie and intimately smoothed the front of his shirt into his waistband. "That's better. I'll just explain you're one of my assistants. You've worked at an event with me before."

"And a bomb went off that time, G."

Ignoring his comment, she looked down at her gold designer watch and pursed her red lips. "It's almost cocktail hour. I have work to do. Follow me. Did I tell you I think I've figured out who the FBI agents are?"

Daniel did as he was told. He felt a headache coming. *How could she possibly uncover who the undercover agents were? I don't want to know.*

It wasn't until they entered the ballroom that professional Ms. Malloy truly appeared. She grabbed her clipboard, pulled a pen out of her bag, and began to complete a final check for tonight's wedding reception. As she walked toward the band to confirm the first songs, her heels clicked on the wood floor.

"That noise." The clicking was joined by a tapping. Gretchen drummed her perfectly red manicured nails on her clipboard as she spoke with the decorator who was adding on the final flower on the cake. By the time she returned to his side, Daniel's headache was raging. "Do you have a couple of aspirin? I have a terrible headache."

"Of course I do." Gretchen dug into her professional bag and pulled out a case. "Here you go, now if you need an allergy pill, I have that too. Bandaids, those little things you put on corns and bunions, cold sore medication, antiseptic, anti-itch, mosquito spray–"

"What the hell?"

Gretchen looked up; her glasses perched on the edge of her nose. "For outside weddings, of course. Do you need something to wash it down?" Magically, a bottle of trendy water appeared.

Daniel threw the pills in his mouth. He stopped prior to swallowing. "Nah, I'm good. What else do you have in that bag?"

"So much. I have flats for when my feet get tired–"

"What?" Daniel looked within it for proof.

"My feet sometimes get very tired. I work very hard."

Daniel pulled out another pair of high heels. This pair was almost like a cheetah print with a gold pattern he couldn't really describe. "And extra heels?"

"Of course, you never know when you might need an extra pair. As you have learned, stilettos can be used to thwart evil. And, as you will discover later in the privacy of our boudoir, dearest, they can be used for good. Good or evil, take your pick." Gretchen winked. She turned away when she heard the bride and groom enter the large ballroom for a peek at the decorations and cake.

Daniel admired the sight. Watching her walk away always changed his mood, only for the better. The sway of her hips and perfect posture held the promise of a long evening once they were home.

"She can use the stilettos for good or evil?" *Exactly what is she going to do with those heels tonight? I can only imagine.*

Daniel Williams began to laugh, loud enough that Gretchen glanced back and wondered if he had lost his mind. And poof, just like that his headache vanished.

You can use stilettos for good or for evil. With you, darling Gretchen Malloy, it's always a little bit of both. Bring either on, and thank God I'm younger than you. If I were older, I'm not sure I could keep up with you and those heels of yours.

What's Next?

It's always a balancing act of some kind when it comes to Gretchen Malloy. Either she's striding perfectly atop a new pair of designer stilettos, or she's discovering who is good and who is evil, and perhaps a little of both. There's the professional Ms. Malloy and the dynamic woman who has finally found the love of her life.

It'll surely be a balancing act for the elite event planner and the detective as they continue their romance and thwart crime in their beloved city.

Never underestimate the benefits of a fine pair of heels!

C.L. BAUER

C.L. Bauer lives in Kansas City, Missouri. Her first novel *The Poppy Drop, A Lily List Mystery* was well received by the top 100 Books of Independent Publishers when it launched in 2018.

The series features the highly organized, post-it note, and list making florist Lily Schmidt. Readers have enjoyed the mysteries and the characters who come in and out of her life. Ms. Bauer draws on true events from her family's wedding and event flower business. With over one hundred years of serving families on their special days, Clara's Flowers has received numerous awards in the wedding world, including "best of" and "legacy winner" for service and design.

With a background in journalism and communication, C.L. Bauer has returned to her first love of writing. Currently, *The Lily List Mysteries and The Exclusive Series* keep her busy. Her upcoming projects include more cozy(ish) adventures with Lily and friends, a memoir of her father's World War II days, a psychological thriller, and a mystery/thriller series based on the history of her hometown.

C.L. Bauer loves to interact with her readers. She'll accept invitations from book clubs for in-person appearances or virtual ones. You can contact her through her pages on Facebook, Instagram, Twitter, Pinterest, Netgalley, and Goodreads.

Join her monthly newsletter by signing up on her website www.clbauer.com or email her at clbauerkc@gmail.com. As always…Happy reading!

Milton Keynes UK
Ingram Content Group UK Ltd.
UKHW030252190324
439698UK00015B/1035